Fledging

ROSE DIELL

RENARD PRESS

RENARD PRESS LTD

124 City Road
London EC1V 2NX
United Kingdom
info@renardpress.com
020 8050 2928

www.renardpress.com

Fledging first published by Renard Press Ltd in 2024

Text © Rose Diell, 2024

Cover design by Will Dady

Printed and bound in the UK on carbon-balanced papers by CMP Books

ISBN: 978-1-80447-089-3

9 8 7 6 5 4 3 2 1

Rose Diell asserts her moral right to be identified as the author of this work in accordance with the Copyright, Designs and Patents Act 1988.

This is a work of fiction. Any resemblance to actual persons, living or dead, is purely coincidental, or is used fictitiously.

CLIMATE POSITIVE Renard Press is proud to be a climate positive publisher, removing more carbon from the air than we emit and planting a small forest. For more information see renardpress.com/eco.

All rights reserved. This publication may not be reproduced, stored in a retrieval system or transmitted, in any form or by any means – electronic, mechanical, photocopying, recording or otherwise – without the prior permission of the publisher.

CONTENTS

Fledging
    Brooding   3
    Hatching   69
    Fledging   155

Acknowledgements   167

FLEDGING

BROODING

It starts as bloating, a hard curvature in my gut that won't go away. I wonder if it's my period, but it isn't the right time. The cramps come slowly at first, like a rising tide, and then grow shorter and sharper, a racing heartbeat.

I press my hands into the kitchen counter and bend over myself, navel-gazing. I wonder if I have any pills left. Mum always tells me to use them only as a last resort. I fill a mug with water, but the medicine shelf's empty.

The cup drops from my hands and rolls on the floor. I groan, rivers running across the linoleum as I clutch at my sides. Over the past few months, I've come to know pain more intimately, but this is something new.

I stagger to the small room at the top of the stairs, unsure whether to sit on the bowl or kneel beside it. It's one of those rooms where nothing fits, the sink overhanging the loo, butting up against a bathtub lined with long-empty bottles of shampoo.

Something's coming, but from where I don't know. My abdomen constricts, invisible hands wringing it like a damp cloth. I fumble with the zip of my jeans, thinking 'fuckfuckfuckfuck' in time with the beats of my speeding heart.

I lean forward, elbows on knees, fingers laced together, eyes closed to shut out the pain. I rock back and forth. And I begin to push.

Something large and smooth is coming out, but not from where I'd expected. It's coming from the empty space between my legs that's always there, the pocket that's as much a part of me as my fingers and toes. No-no-no-no. This can't be happening. Not now.

Frantically, I begin to count. When did I last bleed?

I've been asking myself what I want, going round in circles, questioning again and again. Now I'm terrified my body has got ahead of my brain.

Prematurely.

Somewhere in my head a voice says, *Maybe this is what you want*. The voice sounds like our old neighbour, who'd always give unsolicited advice about how to do our front garden, or which colour to paint our door. But it's quickly drowned out by the rest of my brain screaming, *Not now. Not yet. I need more time.*

Whatever it is, it's rounded and white. I wish I could force it back inside, like choking back vomit. But it seems whatever it is has been festering for too long. My body wants it out. I begin to push, clenching my teeth and digging my fingers into the backs of my hands. A sheen develops on my face. My mind is still screaming – *it can't be, it can't be* – as I will whatever it is back inside. But my body is determined to expel. Expunge.

Bent over, I begin to pray – not to a god but to some dark space inside of me, dredging strength as my jaw muscles start to ache and my abdomen constricts still tighter, squeezing the breath out of me, bringing the first taste of nausea.

Finally, with a deep breath and a last push, something splashes into the water and I feel my whole body give. I sit there, catching my breath, eyes closed, suddenly wondering whether I could stay here for ever, head resting on my knuckles, and never have to face up to whatever's now floating in the bowl. I can't hear anything. I'm not sure whether to be reassured by that or concerned. I remember pink bubble-letter headlines in glossy magazines, girls who didn't even realise they were pregnant. Idiots.

Over the past few months, I've been feeling a weight, my heart dropping into my abdomen and twisting, writhing pain, but it only made me think I should see a doctor, check the kaleidoscope of cancers. Now I ask myself: was it my body preparing for this moment all along?

I feel heat spread across my face, judging myself in the absence of anyone here else to do it.

In the midst of my shame, I begin to wonder. Not looking becomes worse than looking. There's a rusty, salty smell in the air, and I need to put a picture to it before my mind fills in the worst.

As if emerging from wreckage, I allow myself to sit up and open my eyes. I widen my thighs to look down into the water below. A white moon winks back at me from a sea of red.

I yelp, jumping up from the seat, scrabbling for more and more toilet paper to wipe myself and pull my underwear back on. This is impossible – this must be a nightmare. But looking in the mirror at the woman who looks like me, I know it's not. I kneel by the side of the toilet bowl. Clutching the seat as if hanging on for dear life, I allow myself to peer down into its depths. A pale sort of ball, floating in a mess of congealed red gunk and yellow pus. It stares up at me like a bloodshot eye. Accusatory.

I start to wish it was only a baby. Not that there's an 'only' when it comes to babies. I know that – that's why I've been self-dissecting for so long; why I've been the woman they don't show in the adverts, the one crying with relief to see a single line on the test – no virus today. But at least with a baby there are processes to follow. People to call. Options to consider. My options now are—

I turn, and retch into the bin. Acid and bile fill the air. I retch again.

I try to slow my breathing, thinking of the phrase 'compose yourself'. But that always seems to describe the act of slotting back into society, behaving as you should. No one on earth could tell me how I 'should' behave now. As for society…

I stare at the grouting for a minute, but see only the bloodshot eye, unrelenting. I realise I can't stay here on the floor all day. I also realise, with another wave of nausea, that I want to touch it. Perhaps to see if it's real. Or perhaps just to see what it feels like. Carefully, as if wounded, I raise myself to a higher kneel and peer into the gory depths below. Instantly that familiar iron smell rolls through me, laced with something rancid. I grit my teeth and roll up a sleeve to reach my hands into the water. It's disconcertingly warm. I shudder: that's my warmth. I can't help but grimace as my fingers come into contact with the red gelatinous liquid, but it's only my own blood, after all (I tell myself). It's natural (I tell myself).

Fingers splayed across the smooth surface of the object, fingertips bloody, I lift it out of the water just high enough to let the worst of the drips sound ominously into the murkiness below. It's nearly small enough to lift with one hand, but that feels precarious, so I take it in both. I raise it up into the air above me, as if lifting the heavenly host.

It's not an eye at all. It's a perfect oval.

Where the blood has dripped away, its surface is chalky smooth.

It's an egg.

Five months ago. My best friend, the girl I'd eaten crayons with – raised woodlice – spied on family members – made-believe dragons – fake-baked cookies with – told me she was pregnant.

Was it then that the egg first took form?

We were sitting on a bench on London Fields, one towards each end so we could face each other. The fading green of late summer spread out from us towards a line of trees, a border between the park and the blocks of flats beyond. Safa looked on-trend in a striped baggy sweatshirt and biker boots. I was regretting my over-confident summer dress.

'Needed to get on with it,' she was saying. 'Time's running out. If I'm going to have another by the time I'm thirty-seven.' Safa waved her hands around, casually (she thought), frantically (it appeared to me), her striking hazel eyes gleaming. She'd always wanted children – I knew she did. Even when we played our games in our forts there was always a baby involved – but it still came as a surprise. Why now? How now?

'This is huge,' I said, suppressing a shiver.

'Massive,' she said, grinning. There was something manic about the glint in her eyes. 'If it happens. It's still early. But I wanted you to know.'

I'd wondered why she ordered a decaf at the kiosk. Now it all made sense.

I suddenly wondered what her last drink had been.

Did you gorge on sushi and brie before you stopped taking the pill? I wanted to ask.

'I'm happy for you,' I said, and leant in for a hug. I was. Happy it was her, not me. I tried not to hug too hard, suddenly seized of the urge to keep hold of her and never let go. Tried to ignore the little fingers clawing at my throat. Deep breaths. *Think of your yoga videos.*

Pregnant women have to do yoga differently, I thought, looking at her. Their tendons can snap like elastic bands because their pregnant muscles don't know how far they've stretched. Or their pregnant brains. Something like that, anyway. I don't know which.

Suddenly I couldn't think of anything to say. A world of possibilities – trips to plan, restaurants to book, kooky pop-up events to get in line for, drinking games to play – all seemed now reduced into one: her baby. Not one. Not reduced. A baby opens. A baby is an opportunity. Look at the joy in her eyes! Think of the experiences she'll have! You haven't lived until you've been a mother.

You haven't lived.

You haven't known love.

'I'm happy for you,' I said. Deep breaths. First my friend Dimitri, now Safa. Another one bites the dust. My day of reckoning inches nearer.

'You said that already,' she said, giggling. Nervously?

We got up; no need to say anything, but somehow it felt like the right moment to keep walking. We overtook the parents with their toddlers, but lagged behind the cyclists and the roller skaters with their 80s elbow pads. The concrete path snaked through proud tree trunks and past the lido, its squat orange-tiled roof out of place amongst the greenery. We circled almost the whole park talking about *Bake Off* and *Strictly* before I couldn't resist quizzing her again.

I stopped short, turned to her. Children ran past us with their swimming gear, screaming.

'What made you do it?' I asked desperately, thirsty for her answer, fixated on her shining eyes in the hope they really were windows to the soul. 'Take the plunge?' I pictured tentative toes on the concrete edge of the lido, a sudden leap into the unknown, full, blinding immersion, and then surfacing for air. 'Why now?'

'You asked that already too,' she said, moving from giggling to frowning. A small bite of the lip, a little chew, as if on now-banned serrano ham. 'It's time.'

In the bathroom, blood crusting beneath my fingernails and egg held high, I think of David.

I wish I could call him. It must be the middle of the night there. But then I try to imagine the conversation. His mind perceives only straight lines. He'd assume it was a joke. A fantasy. Some kind of metaphor.

I don't blame him. There's no way I'd believe this, not without seeing it with my own eyes. Silly phrase. It's not as if you can ever see through anyone else's, not really, much as we might try. We don't even know if we see the same colours. My red could be your green could be someone else's fuchsia. Maybe that's what happens when I look at a baby. Maybe I'm not seeing something other people see. I'm baby-blind. I only see one colour, and it's a fine one, not bad at all, maybe like a sort of dusky rose, or even a teal, but not the rainbows, the sparkles, the off-the-scale prism exploding in a supernova that others see.

I picture David in front of me, his straight jaw, broad shoulders, floppy hair. That look in his eyes which tells me he's got me all worked out. Except now he's puzzled. This is something even he can't work out.

David, something tragic has happened.

David, I've got something to tell you.

David, I think there's something wrong with me.

David, please don't think I'm crazy.

David, I think I'm imagining things.

I'm crazy. I must be?

Or perhaps *hysterical* is the more appropriate word. What was it Plato called a uterus lacking both a male and a child? *'Sad and unfortunate.'*

I try to calm my thoughts. I find myself thinking of the phrase 'pregnant pause'. It's me and the unavoidable reality of this room: this silent egg, blankly staring me in the face and holding my eyes open so I can't look away. Somewhere beneath the screaming in my brain, my body is also roaring back to life, reminding me that it's there. I feel sore all over, bruised and tender where the egg forced itself on to the world. My arms shake, and for a moment I fear – wish – that the egg will fall to the ground and crack. But I know I can't let that happen; the mere thought sends a rush through my veins. First, I think it's a primal desire to protect this thing, whatever it is. Then I think maybe it's something else: a deep hunger to know what's inside.

Instead, I sink to the floor, clutching the egg to my chest. The sink looms above my head; the bathtub is a blank wall in front of me. And then the cramping returns, softer this time, the echo of a question only half-answered.

Time seems to be running out everywhere I go, sand becoming water and then evaporating before my eyes. A few weeks ago, on the phone with Mum, in the lull between Christmas and New Year. I was in the kitchen, leaning on the counter, half the vegetables chopped for dinner but no cooking started. As soon as I heard her voice, with its remnants of Italian intonation, I could picture her: crinkly eyes, hair tied loosely, a tentative smile.

'The latest prognosis is not good,' she said. 'I can't avoid it any longer: I'm composting, Lia. Not long now before I'm six feet under at the end of your garden.'

I looked at the vegetable cuttings spread over the counter, browning at the edges. We all wilt eventually. But Mum was only sixty-nine.

I told myself she was joking. She'd been saying things like this for a while, for half my life, it seemed – it was in her nature, Sicilian fatalism, she said. I told myself she was exaggerating, had misunderstood. And I decided not to correct her mixed metaphor, though it irked me. Compost sits *above* the ground – in bins, usually.

'Surely there must be something they can do!' I said, contemplating the mysterious 'they', the powers that be, the holders of the elixir of life. Wishing I could track down this 'they', shake them until it hurt. Until they worked out a way to save Mum.

'Maybe. We'll have to see. Can you come over tomorrow?'

I pictured Mum's face – clear blue eyes disappearing into folds of skin, her tissue-paper hands aged by the years, by this disease. The smell of bougainvillea filled my nostrils, and freshly baked sponge, and a cup of tea after a rainy walk. But there was something else, too. Things going stale. Beginning to decay. I tried not to think of her metaphor.

'There's nothing I'd like more,' I said. She sounded surprised, even on the phone. I'm not normally so effusive.

'Are you OK otherwise? How's work going? Your songwriting?' she asked, her voice mum-like, powdered with sugar, trying to deflect attention from herself.

'Perfectly all right,' I said, trying to keep my voice even. The last thing I wanted to do was bring her down. 'It'll be good to see you.'

We hung up and I stared at the unchopped carrots, unable to remember what I was supposed to do with them. My phone screen switched to clock view: the seconds ticked by, and still the carrots lay there, the peel ready for composting.

I looked up, trying to place myself in time and space, and saw the other clock in the room: the old-fashioned one on the wall, with a proud face and angry hands, a nod to the days when such things were needed. Insurance against running out of charge, smashed screens, zombie apocalypses.

We must always know the time, no matter what happens, for if we don't know how much time there is, how will we know how much we have left?

I picked up the knife and began to chop. The next day, I'd go to see Mum.

Tick.

◯

The egg is a bit bigger than a baby's head. I think. No wonder it felt like it was turning me inside out. Imagine giving birth to a whole baby. I think of baby charts, fruit comparisons, blueberries to pomegranates. What size is this? Pineapple? Thank God no prickles. I feel panic rising in my throat. What the fuck is inside?

That's the thing. There's no way of knowing. It could be a lizard, a chick, a salamander – maybe even a dragon, now I come to think of it. Or something I've never heard of. I mean, has a woman ever laid an egg before?

The cramps subside again, and I start to wonder why I'm holding the grim thing. I notice a smudge of blood on the white bathtub edge, wonder how it got there. I curse myself for my clutter: the bubble-bath not needed, the old razor heads I should have thrown away. I clutch the egg against my chest with one hand and use the other to pull myself up to the sink, then stand over it and pause, trying not to look at myself in the mirror. Once again I imagine the egg slipping through my fingers, a fumble that could have been an accident, and falling to the floor so that it cracks into a million pieces and what's left behind is… what?

Something stops me. Perhaps it's the lead in my heart, in my gut. Perhaps it's that I'm already hypnotised by its elliptical nature, bewitched by its smooth white face. Perhaps it's that my brain doesn't want to imagine what I might find inside. Perhaps it's the sense that I've embarked on an adventure and need to see it through.

Carefully, I manoeuvre the egg in the sink so that it's beneath the taps, still avoiding my own reflection, though I know it's there, inches from my forehead. The egg feels heavy, though maybe that's only my shaking arms. Heavy enough for something to be in there, incubating, waiting to come alive. I turn the knobs so that cool water rushes over my hands, then worry that whatever is inside will get too cold, so add some hot, until it's perfectly lukewarm. I cup its round shape in my palms, spreading the water so that all the blood and debris washes away. Now it shines whiter than the sink. I put my jeans back on, take a warm towel from the rack, use it to lift and wrap the egg, and before I know it I'm cradling it, sat on the closed toilet lid, looking down at this mysterious object in my arms that is apparently now my responsibility.

My phone rings from my music room – a little box room the estate agent called the 'nursery'. I jump, and swear as I try to stop myself dropping my bundle. I place it gently on the floor, still wrapped in the towel, and follow the strains of the only song I've ever sold – 'Beyond You' – across the landing. I pull open the door and step over boxes of sheet music, scattered pens and a hoodie in need of a wash to reach my phone, sitting on the control panel of the keyboard. It's Mum.

'How are you, *cara*?'

This contact with the outside world wakes me with a sickening jolt. It's as if I've been in a trance, high on endorphins, and my mother's voice has crashed over me like a bucket of ice. Everything that's just happened flashes before me like a crime-scene montage: taking a break from songwriting because I was starting to feel funny, heading to the kitchen for a snack, then neglecting the snack to press my fist into my stomach, the cramps, the buckling over the toilet, the contractions, the gory mess I've flushed away, this impossible, impossible egg, produced somehow by this body of mine – *Et tu, Brute?* And now my mum's voice on the phone, like bass booming from the subwoofer.

This is not a drill.

'I'm…' I begin, before realising there is nothing I can say. *A reptile?* My sense of humour's intact, at least.

My Simon & Garfunkel poster and the cupboard full of David's old DVDs feel as if they're closing in, the world shrinking around me. I'm suffocating. I need to get out. I throw my phone down on the little keyboard stool, turn and run, wincing, trying to ignore my sore joints and the raw feeling in my knickers. Down the stairs, out the front door. It slams behind me, heavy in the night air.

My breath mists in the January cold. People have put out their rubbish and their recycling, council logos emblazoned on green and purple plastic. The notion that the sacred rhythm of Bin Night still continues seems so absurd, I almost break into laughter. But then I register the words 'free range' on an empty egg carton and the thought that I could abandon the egg in one of these crates like a foundling becomes too-too-tempting. I need to get away from this preposterous ordinariness, from my preposterous thoughts. I start to run, feet sounding out like slaps in the silence.

Blocks of flats tower over me from the other side of the road, while on my side the terrace of seventies box houses stretches down the hill, each of the glowing windows signalling at least one oblivious person going about their entirely ordinary evening, eggs only relevant to their chocolate mousse or Victoria sponge. I know the faces behind many of the curtains; unusually for this city, David and I have got to know them since moving in. 'At least we've got people to call in an emergency,' we've said to each other on several occasions. But if I am sure of one thing, it is that I will not be calling anyone.

I run past house after house, familiar curtains blurring until I reach the houses that are only houses and carry no reference or meaning.

I've been feeling lightheaded, dizzy, but the cold air starts to revive me. My breath puffs silver, but I don't care. My feet pound against the pavement and I start to sweat, despite not taking a jacket. I run past leering men and shivering schoolchildren still in their uniforms, gleefully starting their weekends. I dash across a road, narrowly missed by a screeching Golf. Run away from the station, up the hill this time. Up, up and up until my heart's going to explode. I keep running until I reach the top, where there's a gap in the buildings and you can see the whole of London stretched out before you. In the past this view has inspired me, set new tunes playing in my head. But tonight I only see indistinguishable lights rising from white noise. All the sounds of the street have combined into one raucous mass, and the city is unending.

I feel sobs building in my chest, like an electric kettle ready to boil. I look around at the bus stop, the Victorian townhouses, the turreted roof of the Horniman museum silhouetted against the city, wonder how I got here. Try to organise my thoughts. Running away won't fix anything. The egg will still be there when I get home. OK, I could keep running for ever, invent an alias, get a new life, join a witness-protection programme. I think of Victoria coach station, the place Safa and I always said we'd go if we needed to run away: screens announcing the names of cities five days' ride from here, numbered door after numbered door, queues of people, the buses waiting like mastodons in the forecourt, ready to make their slow lumbering progress under the English Channel and off across the continent.

But none of that makes any sense. I have Mum to think of. David, thousands of miles away on his months-long orchestra fellowship, the opportunity of a lifetime. My keyboard. My home. Besides, I have an image of the egg somehow finding me wherever I go, having to repeat the whole laying experience, perhaps – the cramps and the nausea and the blood – only to be confronted by the same white face.

I swoon, grab a bollard to steady myself. With a sense of the inevitable I force myself to turn back, walking now as my heart rate slows. My feet move automatically, like cogs in a wheel, but at the same time drag as if fighting magnetic repulsion. The thought of what's waiting at home is terrible, but at the same time I want nothing else but to return. I reach my street. Terraces line the road on either side, their uniformity underlining their indifference. Finally, I'm standing outside my house, counting my breaths, trying to talk myself into going in, burning with both curiosity and dread, like the time we went to see my music teacher's open casket. It's hard to believe how ordinary my house looks. If it were an imposing Edwardian, majestic Georgian or august Victorian, perhaps I could just about believe that something impossible had happened inside. But looking at the flat façade with its seventies weatherboard and hanging red tiles, I can almost convince myself that nothing's happened at all. That I've imagined the whole thing.

Except, deep down, I know that I haven't.

I drag my feet up the path towards the poky porch. Time for my suburban nightmare to pick up where it left off.

I reach for the white plastic door handle, try to turn it.

I'm locked out.

My legs give way; I no longer have the strength to stand, and I'm crying tears which warm my frosty cheeks, while my fingertips and buttocks in their thin leggings turn to ice.

My next-door neighbour has our key. She's the first person we spoke to on the street; invited us for tea when we first moved. Now I do her shopping once a week, and sometimes pop in to play for her on the piano.

I push myself up from the cold stony ground. I force my aching muscles to her front door, which looks the same as mine, like every door on the street. I ring the bell. I can picture the egg, find myself hoping that it's all right. What seems like an age passes while my shivers build and anxiety clamours in my chest. Finally, I see a light coming on in the hall, make out a shuffling figure through the floral frosted glass. Mary opens the door, her wrinkled face a question mark below her helmet of tight ringlet curls. She wants to chat. 'You look a bit flushed, dear.'

I rush her. 'So sorry – I'm locked out; could I get my key? Sorry to interrupt your evening.'

She looks alarmed by my haste; I use the cold as an excuse, hopping from one foot to another.

'Hope everything's OK,' she says, meaningfully, as if the words are in italics. Ordinarily seeing her would make me feel calm, make everything solid. But today I need to get into my house with the urgency of someone about to lose control of their bladder; someone who, like me, cannot trust their own body to keep it together. I need to know that the egg is all right. That nothing has happened to it. That it's still there in the bathroom, in my old white towel, white against white against white.

She rummages in a mahogany bureau near the door for a few moments, then extracts the key, dangling it from the treble-clef keychain I must have given her.

I take it as quickly as I can without snatching it, hurry a thank-you and yet another 'sorry' from the side of my mouth, and rush back to my door, guilty but revived. The key stumbles in the lock but then catches. The door handle gives. Mary's watching to check I've got in safely; I give her a determinedly cheery wave, and catch no more than a glimpse of her waving back as I scramble over the threshold, not bothering to kick off my shoes. My heart pounds as I thud up the stairs.

It's there, a perfect oval. Eternal, self-perpetuating.

The relief of finding it safe is accompanied by the sudden urge to eat. I've forgotten to have dinner, and now all I can think about is a rare steak, oozing scarlet, something I can get my teeth into. I leave the egg in the bathroom, for lack of a better place to put it, and hurry down to the kitchen, a small strip of light in my dark house. But I open the fridge, and funnily enough there are no Michelin stars waiting there. A half-eaten packet of frankfurters will have to do. Two minutes in the microwave later and their smoky meat is burning the roof of my mouth.

I return to the bathroom and sit, cradling the egg in the bath; I lose several hours to terrified wondering, and then it's gone midnight and exhaustion hits me like a double-decker bus. Going to sleep almost seems too ordinary, but for lack of a better idea, I take the egg into the bedroom.

'I guess it's you and me, now,' I say, as I tuck it under the covers, hoping it's not till death do us part. I can't put my finger on it, but there's something familiar about the egg. Perhaps it's because I've been carrying it for some time.

For hours, I lie in the shadows beside the egg, time running on through two and three and four. Funny how what seems like darkness when you first turn off the lights can soon become an unbearable glow from the perpetual light of the city. What was blackness is now my nightstand, the photo of us laughing together on stage, David's suit hanging on the back of the door.

My eyelids are heavy, but the egg is luminous and it won't let me sleep. I try counting sheep, but all I see are eggs flying over stiles. I try my usual technique of shutting each of my thoughts up into a little wooden chest with a big metal padlock, but all I see are eggs. I try mental Post-it notes, scrunching them up and throwing them in the bin, but the egg won't let itself be forgotten.

Finally, exhaustion takes over. 'What will people think…?' I murmur as I drift off to sleep.

Except they won't think anything. Because I'll never, never tell them.

◯

Saturday. A break from PRINCE2 and spreadsheets. When I joined Pentatonic Productions, I thought I'd be working with the artists, midwifing their work from arpeggio to album – not overseeing IT transitions and pay-scale standardisation.

Perhaps it's not that this job is worse than any other. Perhaps I'll always feel apathetic about anything that takes me away from my songwriting. Anything that gets in the way of getting more songs released, going beyond 'Beyond You', which didn't make it anywhere near the charts.

I do have a second passion: the weekend. When my alarm goes off, I do the obvious: snooze, snooze and snooze again. Mum would say I'm lazy. But I'm a firm believer in life's simple pleasures. During the week, the insomnia of indecision has been leaving me empty-eyed and hollow. But at the weekend I make up for lost hours. Today, I drift in and out, a candy-floss sleep that weighs down my eyes and makes my bed the warmest, safest place in the world. I sleep for hours, years, until finally the room is so filled with daylight I can't resist leaning an arm across to open the curtain and reveal a cyan sky. Egg next to me looks cyan too. 'Good morning,' I say to it, and then wonder how long it will be until they institutionalise me.

Though I miss knowing David's somewhere in the house, I still love the feeling of a Saturday morning to myself. Pyjamas, coffee, newspaper. A lined notepad for jotting down song ideas, interesting phrases from the columns. My phone to hand to quick-record any tunes that tiptoe into my head.

But today I don't feel quite so relaxed. The egg has me on edge; I can almost hear it ticking, a bomb ready to go off. For now, I've brought it into the kitchen and perched it in a red bowl on the counter. Like an easter egg. After all, perhaps the Easter Bunny and I have something in common. We're equally implausible.

My phone buzzes. It's woodlice-and-crayon friend, Safa. She wants to go out for dinner – 'While I still can.'

I consider the egg. It attracts and repulses me at the same time. I need to give myself something else to think about. With a kind of mad hope that if I go on as normal, normality will resume, I reply.

We agree to meet at seven o'clock. It's twelve thirty, and I've just finished breakfast. Six and a half hours with the egg stretch ahead of me. I make another coffee, taking more time over it than usual; sit back down at the counter where my newspaper is spread out, the narrow room slowly brightening as a little sunlight comes in through the window.

I've never been one to mind being on my own, and I've never talked to myself. But for some reason I end up talking to the egg. It's hard to describe, but it has a sort of presence. It's impossible to ignore. No matter where in the house I am, I'm drawn back to it.

I've put my hands around it several times, leant in, pressed an ear. Listening for whale song, checking for tremors that might tell me what's inside. Then checked again. But so far all I've noticed is that it was warmer in bed with me last night than it is now. It was warmer when it first came out (did it really come out of *there*?) than it is now.

'Eggcellent,' I say, smiling to myself. 'Dinner with Saffy, before she pops. And then I'll never hear from her again.' I'm only half joking.

Suddenly, I jump up from my stool. The image of a chicken coop, and eggs in incubators come to mind. I rush over to the egg in its red stand on the counter. It's colder still.

Bugger.

'Fuckety fuck,' I say, and hug the egg to myself, trying to warm it while my eyes search the room for a longer-term solution. 'Look, Humpty Dumpty, I can't stay here with you all day. Got to go to a restaurant. Got dinner plans.'

My eyes rest on the tea towels. But they're not very thick.

Oven? No, don't want mystery frittata. Even worse than mystery meat.

Finally, I settle on gathering together towels and throws and arranging them in a ring beside the radiator in the living room. I place the egg in the centre. I stand up, pleased with myself, hands on hips. And then it hits me what I'm looking at and my mouth falls open.

I've made a nest.

I look down at my hands. I can't help but think of the old adage about hairy palms. But this time I'm looking for feathers. My heart is pounding and my ears are ringing. I start searching every part of my body with my fingers, rolling up sleeves and trouser legs and peering down the top of my pyjamas. I've laid an egg, I've made a nest, the only logical conclusion is…

But I'm still one-hundred per cent human – at least, as much as I've ever been. Pure mammalian skin, some of it hairier than I'd like. Not a feather or scale in sight. I force myself to slow my breath, lie down on the carpet, Shavasana, Ohmmmm… After a few minutes I feel almost normal. I get up, decide to go upstairs for a shower and catch sight of myself in the hallway mirror. My hair is sticking up in odd directions. My eyes look almost crossed, as if I don't know whether I'm coming or going. But I'm *definitely* human.

'Don't be ridiculous,' my reflection tells me. 'Women don't turn into birds.'

Women don't lay big white eggs, either.

I decide to go running, properly this time, rather than in a post-laying panic. But once I've dug out my leggings, socks, shoes, hat, gloves, got changed and got myself outside, I suddenly become aware that my muscles are barely holding themselves together, and my abs ache with the memory of exertion. So I walk instead, and while I walk I wonder what kind of bird I'd like to be, given the choice. It'd have to be a bird that could fly, of course. Imagine being a kiwi, or an ostrich! The squibs of the avian world. It's normal to think of eagles, with their connotations of grandeur, for soaring great heights. But I'd prefer a swallow. They make me think of summer.

Birds of a feather flock together, I think, and then realise I'm smiling to myself. A walker gives me an odd glance. I try to rearrange my face. It doesn't do to smile in public, not when you're alone. You're supposed to look miserable. So that every man you pass can tell you to cheer up.

I've reached the far end of the park, and normally I'd cross over into the next one. The sycamores there are some of the tallest in London, and I love how overgrown the paths are, even before spring has broken. It's fertile ground for inspiration, melodies mingling in the moss. But without meaning to, I'm worrying about the egg. What if the radiator isn't warm enough, and I've let winter get to the heart of whatever's inside? What if it's so warm that the egg is hatching right now, and I'm missing it while I stomp along this pavement? I turn back, picking up pace as I picture cracks beginning to form on the surface of the egg, earthquakes fracturing its serenity.

But when I tiptoe through the front door fifteen minutes later, the nest, and the egg, are exactly as I left them: unwelcome and somehow unexpected as uninvited house guests who let themselves in while I was out. The living room is incongruously undisturbed around them: slightly saggy sofa, wing-back armchair, overstuffed magazine rack and two higgledy-piggledy bookshelves just getting on with existing like they always have. I find myself sitting cross-legged on the carpet, staring Matilda-like at the eggshell, almost willing it to crack so that I can find out what's inside, questions swirling in my head, asking myself whether I should just Make It Go Away.

When I look at my phone again, I'm astonished to find almost two hours have passed.

I shake off my reverie with an involuntary shoulder roll and toss of my head, and go to my music room: keyboard, recording equipment, notepad, paper. I improvise a few notes, feeling for a tune – close my eyes, try to hear a song taking shape; experiment with different intervals, first stroking the keys and then leaning into them so the sounds which ring out are confident and clear. But the notes remain notes, random words that don't form sentences. And when I look down at my blank music sheet, all I see are little eggs with little arms and legs, tap-dancing on the stave.

When it's time to go I stand in front of the egg again, urging its mystery to be revealed. My decision to meet Safa now seems reckless. How can I leave this thing here, unattended, with no idea what's inside and whether it's about to hatch? I could come back to anything – I could come back to no home at all. I ask myself what David would do. I fish my phone from my pocket, start to type 'I'm really sor—' but then shake my head, shove it back and leave the house as quickly as I can before I have time to change my mind.

A bumpy bus ride later, I meet Safa at a restaurant that's squeezed in twice as many diners as they have space for. We're hunched over a low wooden table, further apart than we should be because Safa's belly keeps her distant; she's expanding, like a balloon slowly filling with air.

I know it's a common complaint that strangers like to pat pregnant bellies, but I feel no urge. Instead, I'm thinking that Safa is no longer a woman; she has become a different species. Or rather, something unnatural. An alien. I know this is completely illogical. Some would say she's more a woman than me. One that I can't relate to, can't imagine being. I feel a kind of dissociation just looking at her. I try to imagine going about my day with that bump, that round egg attached to my front. The irony is bitter-tasting.

'I'm turning into Moby Dick,' she grins. 'And the way I walk, I'm more a penguin than a person!'

But this is natural to her. A mark of pride. Even when she feels bloated and her ankles swell, it's OK. Something is coming. Something which will make it all worth it. I can see it in her brown eyes, where, as the expression goes, the baby already twinkles.

'How are you feeling? Have you had much morning sickness?' I ask. 'How was the last scan?'

I can tell she wants to move the subject on to something else, doesn't want to make it all about her, but it's the only thing the two of us can think about. I'm hungry for every detail, cataloguing them in my mind, sifting the pros from the cons. Her child doesn't need to be born to demand all our attention.

I picture myself sitting on her side of the table, try to feel her excitement, imagine new life inside me: the tremolo of a butterfly. But all I feel is dread, and the egg is there again as an eye, gaze unbroken, boring into my soul.

Then, 'But how are *you* doing?' she asks, eyes wide with sincerity, leaning across the table towards me. 'How's work – did you manage to get a project that's a bit more exciting?'

For a mad moment I think of telling her about the egg. Then I have the foresight to imagine the conversation, and stop myself just in time. She'd probably think I was joking, just like David would, making some strange reference. I wonder how it's doing, wonder if I left the heat on, hope it doesn't crack while I'm here, at this vegetarian restaurant, eating sweet-potato fries and sipping white wine. Is that because I feel protective over it, want to be there to coddle whatever hatches? Or because I can't bear the thought of missing it, waiting any longer to find out what's inside, or not finding out at all – just returning to an empty shell?

I have a mad urge to rush home, to sit in front of the egg again, to let these restless thoughts run their course. But I know this is one of my last chances to see Safa. I decide to stay.

'Oh, you know, the usual. Work is still work; nothing exciting to report. Did the soup kitchen again last week. Jess and I were thinking of a day trip to Bath, if you want to come?' (Bath now seems an impossibility, ever since the egg appeared; Safa only smiles – too close to term.) 'Oh – and I saw this great gig in Camden, really original stuff – inspired me to write a new track, actually!'

It all feels like gloating, somehow, when she's so immobile, and yet I know she doesn't want me to think that way, and I don't know what else to say. I order one glass of wine, and then another. I drink to fill the silences. I can see Safa getting tired. The couple at the table too close to ours gets up to go.

Safa looks as if she might suggest we follow suit. I think that perhaps I'll use what's left of the evening to compose a few more bars of the piece I'm working on.

But then I remember the egg, and suddenly I'm sure I don't want to go home. I think of our first day at uni together (we arranged to go to the same one), before we'd met Jess; how Safa cracked one of her jokes to stop me feeling nervous and then offered me one of her mum's pistachio cookies. I want to hug Safa tight and never let go.

This time is too precious. The night is too young, and so are we. Safa's free – though I know I shouldn't see it that way – for one more month.

'Let's go dancing!' I cry out, a little more loudly than I'd intended. The diners on the other side of us stare at me ever so briefly. The egg glimmers dimly in the corners of my mind, but I force it further into the shadows. I need this.

'Are you joking?' she asks, gesturing towards her belly.

'You're right,' I mutter. We pay up and exit to the cold and bright lights of Drury Lane, where tourists, students and Londoners on their way to a night's entertainment mingle and merge on the pavement.

'That was lovely,' says Safa cheerfully. I can see she's wrapping up the night, ready to head home to her husband. I can see that I've lost, and the thought of going home fills me not with curiosity but with dread.

At that moment I spot a familiar face across the road, the randomisation matrix of the city throwing up one of those coincidences it delivers from time to time, gold and crunchy as a Ferrero Rocher. It's Meg!

Meg, who's always up for it. Meg, who's always good value. Meg, who will have you taking shots within half an hour and have you out until three in the morning. In contrast with Safa, who's tall, willowy and tawny-skinned, Meg is short, stout and china-doll pale, with jet-black hair that tonight is pulled into a messy bun spilling out of the hood of her long, quilted coat.

'Looks like your evening's sorted,' says Safa sardonically, as if she's past all of this, too mature now, already the grandmother she'll one day be.

I call out to Meg. Her cheeks dimple when she sees us and she rushes over, teetering a little on heeled ankle boots.

'Went for a glass of wine and ended up on mojitos!' she exclaims. We hug, her coat pillowing around me. She and Safa do the same. 'What are you two up to, then?' Meg asks.

'Just heading home, actually,' Safa says, stifling a yawn. Then, more brightly: 'So lovely to see you, though!'

Meg gives me a playful look, almost as if she's winking, though her eyes are wide open. 'Come on, Safa, one little mocktail can't hurt!' she says with an ironic smile.

Safa just gestures at her bump again. 'You know I'd love to.'

'Come on, let the poor girl go home,' I say, putting my arm around Safa's shoulders. I can tell she's exhausted.

I give Safa the tightest hug I can muster – *don't leave me, I love you* – and she heads for the Tube.

'Right, what now?' says Meg, grinning. There's a different kind of twinkle in her eyes. It's the twinkle of possibility.

I think of the egg for a moment. Then I think of Safa's belly, the same shape.

'Fuck it,' I say. The phrase to end all phrases. The card to get out of jail free. The pin coming out of the grenade. Tonight is the only night that matters. YOLO. Carpe diem.

Meg takes my hand, drags me into the nearest pub. There's a crush inside, voices bouncing off the ceiling. 'Shots?' she says, grinning wickedly.

The rest of the evening unfolds like a montage in a badly scripted teen movie. We're shooting stars, spinning on every axis. We do the shots, sing the songs, dance as if the world is ending. We hug each other tight and tell each other we'll always be friends. We go our separate ways, we stagger home.

I don't even check in on the egg nesting in my front room as I stumble up to bed. That is to say – I pause, ever so briefly, swaying a little (maybe), outside the living-room door. I almost stick my head in. And then I think better of it. Tomorrow's another day.

No disaster befalls the egg. In the morning it's still there, intact, wrapped in blankets. I lie on the carpet, embracing my hangover, and put my hands around it, lift it to place a cheek against the rough surface. It's warm, though maybe because it's been next to the radiator.

Feeling slightly nauseous, I wonder if I should have followed Safa's example, and gone home at a more civilised hour. Surely an adult shouldn't lie on the floor like this on a Sunday morning. My friend Jess wouldn't do this – she'd want to do something more 'productive'.

'Is it time I grew up?' I ask the egg. They said bleeding made girls into women. They said marriage made you whole. At my age, the ask is to be reproductive. I ask the egg: 'Am I being reductive?'

I wonder if whatever's inside can hear. I think about mothers playing Mozart to the unborn. I get up, turn on my speakers, select a playlist called 'Classical Music Bangers'.

As Symphony No. 5 fills the room (*dun-dun-dun-duh!*), I suddenly wonder: how do I know whatever's in there is still alive? An egg, after all, is a sort of puzzle. You can't know what's inside unless you crack it (pun intended... maybe I do have baby brain), and if you do that, well, it's far too late.

Maybe there's nothing inside it at all. It might be nothing more than a hollow shell, already sucked dry by the proverbial grandmother.

(*Dun-dun-dun-duh!*)

In that case, all I can do is wait for a bad smell.

I work from home and in the evening, I visit Mum. Her house is one of those where life overflows from every nook and cranny. Even the plants in the front garden are trying to escape their pot and trellis prisons, rambling over the doorway, overhanging the windows and cracking the path. The hallways are filled with boxes, ready to be unpacked or packed up – I never know which. The shelves have double rows of books, and trinkets cover every surface, and each room seems to have its own pile of newspapers, its own bag for the charity shop and its own collection of family portraits. So many family portraits. People that many wouldn't even consider family – second and third cousins, several times removed, people we call family but aren't even related to.

She's sitting in her easy chair, a sepia version of her normal self. Her hair flows loose down her shoulders, but what was once liquid silver is now turning to flax. Her wide blue eyes, once diamonds, are misted windowpanes. Even her voice sounds distant, her usually heavy consonants flattened somehow, as if reaching me through muslin. I sit beside her, hold her hand; I think that perhaps if I squeeze tight enough, I'll be able to anchor her to this world, prevent her slipping into the next. Once she would have cracked a joke or launched into a story about her most recent meet-up with one of her many friends. Instead, she strokes my hair gently, as if I were a child.

'It's so nice to see you,' she says, like she always does. I wonder if she'll go further this time, make some big avowal of how I'm the most important thing that ever happened in her life, how I saved her, gave her life meaning. But this isn't a film, and she doesn't.

'It's nice to see you too,' I say, and I want to go further, say that I can't imagine living without her, that she made me, and made me who I am, that I want to put her in a jar and slam the lid on so she can never escape. But it feels like enough.

We sit in silence for a while. I'm aching to tell her about the egg, with an intensity that's almost painful – so that she can take me in her arms and tell me everything's going to be OK, that there's a simple explanation for everything in this life.

She offers me a cup of tea, which I make, of course, because I know how much energy it would cost her to get up.

She smiles at me as she drinks it, steam rising before her sky-blue eyes. It seems to me that the universe is in those eyes – not just twinkling stars, but whole galaxies, containing everything I've ever known, or ever will. I can't help but think of the way she used to scoop me up when I'd had a fall, cradle me over her shoulder and sing me one of her Sicilian folk songs: '*Vinni la primavera*', spring has come. That was before even a chipped yellow mug became an effort to lift.

I try to think of a question to ask her. Not *Are there platypuses in our family tree?* but something heartfelt and real. Something I haven't asked before, something that will give me an insight into her, the person before the mother, capture her and put her behind glass. She already looks like parchment; she already looks pickled. Is there nothing more I can glean?

'When was your first date?' I ask her. She smiles.

'You've asked me that before.'

Of course I have. I should have recorded her answers.

'What about Grandma's?' I ask. I suddenly understand that if I lose Mum, I won't only be losing her, but also everyone in these photo frames who has died – everyone in these photo frames I never got the chance to meet. Everything I'll ever know about them, I have to learn now.

'Let's not talk about Nonna right now.' Her habitual response. Over the years, what I've found out about my grandmother I've had to piece together into the faintest of melodies, from only the timbre and key of what my mother has said, without ever hearing the individual notes.

'Are you glad you had me?' I ask, and then sense that's not the right question. Could any mother answer in the negative to her child? Sure enough, she puts down her tea, reaches out her hand and grabs mine, squeezing it warm and tight. The way she looks at me, I have the sense that if she were stronger she'd come to sit next to me, and take me in her arms. Instead: 'I love you more than anything, Lia.'

I know I should savour the moment, store up these precious seconds together, but my mind keeps running on and my mouth runs with it; a refrain that started long before the egg arrived and has only intensified with its laying.

'Do you think it's a mistake not to have children?'

She pauses, looks at me quizzically. 'There are other things in life, it's true. But raising you has brought me so much joy. And the more I think about the day I'll no longer be here' – I look away, unable to hold her gaze – 'I'm glad to feel I've passed something on to the next generation. A part of myself, in you. This house… my plants.'

It's true, she loves her plants almost like children, some of them decades old. I look around at the walls. I know she painted them herself, saw her do it when I was still in Mary Janes, her hair tied back in a floral bandana and her dungarees flecked with white. I look at the bookshelves, each book dog-eared and love-worn, a collection built steadily over years.

'You could give the house to charity,' I say. 'Donate it to a children's home.' I think of the kids my friend Dimitri and I used to work with, at the youth club.

She looks confused. Her brow furrows. I feel terrible – I'm stuck in my own head, not reacting the way I should.

'Don't you want it?'

'Of course. Yes. No – wait, that's not what I meant,' I say. 'I'm here, after all. I meant, if I wasn't? Would you do it all over again?'

Her eyes widen and she seems to be searching for something in mine.

'Lia, before you arrived, I didn't even know where I was going.'

I return home. Not to my keyboard but to the egg, a blank space in my living room.

BROODING

We've discussed it – of course we have – David and I. A chilly November weekend in Whitstable just before he went away, plimsolls sliding over pebbles while seagulls cawed overhead and the mouth of the Thames yawned in the distance.

In front of a cottage painted blue he blurted it out, boxy in a long black coat, chestnut hair flapping in the bracing sea air: 'Have you made up your mind? About children?'

I found myself wondering how long it had been stoppered inside, whether this was what he had been thinking of while we slurped rock oysters, froze our fingers hunting for cockles (putting the shells back afterwards, mindful of erosion) and pitied a one-legged seagull.

'Maybe just one or two wouldn't be such a game changer. One could fit into your life, I think. There's lots of stuff you could keep doing, like before.' He allowed his face to betray nothing, straight lines as always, master of his emotions.

Do you mean 'you' as in 'me', or 'you' as in 'us'? I wanted to ask.

Easy for you to say, I wanted to say.

Do you want your stomach to stretch like that bulging sail over there, then feel your body pushed to its limit? Do you want to be the factory providing food on demand for however many weeks? Do you want to change permanently, to risk complications (what a word!), depression, a maelstrom of hormones whirling through your mind?

Maybe I'll do that, and then you can promise to take it whenever I want to go out, I thought of saying.

Maybe I'll do that, and you can be the one to leave work and collect it from nursery when it's got the flu, I thought of saying.

That's unfair. He'd be a good father. I can tell he would, even though I have no reference point from which to work: I've never known mine, nor, perhaps unusually, felt the need.

'Would it break your heart if we didn't?' I asked.

'Not as long as I'm with you.' And then came the smile, the cheeks crinkling just for me. My heart crinkling along too, hoping and hoping it was true.

We kept walking, the ebb and flow of the estuary whispering beside us. I squeezed his hand; he squeezed mine back. Morse code. I tried to imagine us on a summer evening with a small child running beside us: her eager eyes, her feet dancing in the waves, the knowing smiles David and I would exchange as she called out to us, singing a song we'd written for her, together. It would be beautiful, in its own way. But it wouldn't be the same. And then we'd get home, and instead of wine, candles and carbonara, there'd be SpaghettiOs, CBeebies and bath time. Maybe an argument about school waiting lists. *The Gruffalo* instead of Austen, then ballet lessons instead of the Royal Albert Hall. Nowhere to hide.

'I still don't know,' I said, and we continued along the shore. But as the waters started to recede, I suddenly understood what the waves were taking with them: my time to decide, with each changing of the tides.

A few days later and I start to wonder if I should go to the doctor. I'm in a peculiar limbo, getting used to having the egg around – if you can say that – going to work, leaving it to see Mum, to do next door's shopping and my own. But

I'm still wondering, constantly, whether it's going to hatch. And why it's here.

It's clearly not normal, what's happened. So, getting a medical opinion would seem the natural thing to do. But every time I imagine the scene, all I see is how ridiculous it would be.

'Doctor, I've given birth to an egg.'

'You must be yolking…' this male doctor in my mind says, tugging at a beard which probably shouldn't be allowed for hygiene reasons.

Or, 'Yes, a simple case of bird flu—'

Or, 'Just your regular Reptile Dysfunction.'

Hardly.

And yet my pains haven't gone away. Maybe it's the after-effects of the laying, but I can still feel a subtle ache most of the time, sitting low in my abdomen, like period pain, and occasionally, a sharper pang from somewhere deeper within, reminding me that I have a womb.

I sit beside the nest, staring at the blank face of the egg. It gives nothing away. I don't *think* whatever's inside will be able to breathe fire; it doesn't feel that way. I put my hand on the egg, and it's tepid – a word I've always hated, but there's no better way to describe its wan temperature: warm enough to be alive, but cold enough that you have to pay attention to sense it. I close my eyes. My heart slows. Breathe in, breathe out. Five more breaths. I imagine my mind is white as the egg. *What are you?* I try to say through my fingers, imagining the message passing through the shell like a golden light to reach whatever's inside, music notes pulsating to the beat.

With a gasp I notice the curtains aren't properly closed. Anyone could walk past and see not just these messy towels, this woman draped over, but also this precious egg, its whiteness shining now in a ray of winter sun, brilliant and untouched. I hurry to close them, and when I do it strikes me, as it has from time to time before I've shaken the thought away, how unusual this must be. The woman who laid an egg. I can picture the headlines now. I once read about a woman who gave birth to rabbits in Victorian times, over a hundred years ago, rabbit after rabbit after rabbit. But it was all a hoax. And they were all stillborn. She was hiding them up there, can you believe it? And the doctor was in on it.

I didn't hide anything. No doctor here.

I resolve to go, after all. I ring up, manage to get an 'emergency' appointment, miraculously, for the next morning. I press my hand to the tepid shell and tuck the towels as closely around it as I can.

I sing, plucking words and notes from the air:

> *We'll find a way, we'll make it through…*
> *Just you and me, just me and you…*

That evening I decide to tell David. I need to share this secret with someone. It's blistering, like all secrets, and I feel as if exposing it to the light is the only way to make it dry up and go away, except the egg is too solid for that.

I'm curled up beneath my duvet, the egg downstairs, in the vain hope that out of sight will be out of mind. As I call David, I can feel the words thronging in my throat, almost tumbling over each other in their enthusiasm to spill out of my mouth.

And then I hear his voice, all the way from Japan. 'Lia?'

Solid, rich like oak. Imbued with reason. A voice that silences clamour and stills my trembling. My mind stops its fluttering from branch to tangled branch and instead marches slowly, stately forward. I find myself relaxing into the sound, the conversation. I ask how his fellowship tour is going. I tell him about my pains.

'Go to the doctor, Lia. Please. For me.'

'I'm booked,' I say, but part of me wonders if it was the egg all along, if the pain will go away now it's laid.

'How's your songwriting? You seemed to be struggling before I left.'

'I've been busy…'

The mere thought of what's been making me busy sets my heart at double time, and I desperately try to refocus on the grain of his voice, to calm the racing, lull myself back into safety. It works. And then I know I can't, won't, do anything to disrupt this. I wallow in its embrace. I imagine his arms around me, feel I could drift into sleep.

All I'm thinking of is David, and his orchestra tour on the other side of the world, and his solid shoulders and steady arms and the sound his cello makes when he plays.

By the time the call has ended I'm curled in a foetal position, sheltered from the world, floating.

I sit at the keyboard in my office. A few hours of work, then my doctor's appointment.

I press Enter, and then Enter again. One chart is replaced with another. Process models squiggle across the page, workstreams and milestones coming together into one orchestrated whole. We'd been meeting the project deadlines, but this week they've slipped. You might say I've had other things on my mind. I open a new email, start to type a falsely cheery salutation. I explain why the email is late. I write the whole thing, hit spellcheck, and then send.

Only after I've sent it do I notice it's addressed to Mr Egg, Esq.

◯

When I was fifteen and preparing for my exams, Mum sat me down in the living room, as overflowing as it is now, and said she had something difficult to tell me.

'I hope you understand how hard it is for me to say this,' she said, biting her lip. I couldn't quite fathom the expression on her face: was it shame? Fear? Her cheekbones seemed pulled back, her mouth thinning, those surprising blue eyes I've inherited wide open and trembling.

My mind started to sift the possibilities, cycling through them as if round the wheel on Mum's old Rolodex. By this point in my life plenty of friends had suffered the trauma of seemingly happy parents suddenly announcing they were getting divorced. Mum had never been with my father at all, so that couldn't be it; others had been ordered to get Saturday jobs, but I'd already told Mum I wanted one; others had... Wait. Some had moved away. Perhaps that was it. Some had been jerked rudely from their familiar existence of friends and Saturdays in the park and gossiping outside the school gates, because of a parent changing jobs or needing to move closer to grandparents, or in some cases, saving for retirement. Was that what Mum was going to say?

Already I started to imagine what that would be like. It would depend where we were going, of course. Moving to another city, Manchester, maybe, was one thing (I had never actually been to Manchester but had a vague idea of it in my head as a smaller, rainier, smokier London, where people's vowels went on twice as long and their hearts were twice as big). In a city you could make friends. There were things to do. Music shops, probably. Concerts, even. Trains, so you could pop back to see people if you really wanted to. If you really missed them.

Moving to 'The Middle of Nowhere', as my Londoner friends and I collectively called anywhere that wasn't walking distance from a shop, was another story. We knew what moving to 'TMON' meant. It meant never seeing each other again, ever. It meant sheep, and the sickly-sweet smell of manure lingering wherever you went. It meant strange barn parties where farmer kids who'd never seen Big Ben got drunk on moonshine and did inexplicable things like tipping cows.

I bit my lip. My whole body tensed. What would I tell Safa?

'Lia, are you listening to me?' Mum said. 'This is important.' The word 'exasperated' came to mind. I wondered if one day I could build a song around that word; I was thinking in lyric and melody even then. It didn't have a very musical sound, not like 'onomatopoeia' or 'lustrous', but it was satisfying. Ex*as*perated.

'*Lia!*' Mum again. 'Will you listen to me for once?'

'Sorry,' I mumbled. The stench of manure filled the air. This was the moment.

'We're going to have to stop your piano lessons,' she said.

This had not even crossed my mind. I was crestfallen. Another good word, usually, but one that brought pain today.

Suddenly, the conversation switched to minor key. I wasn't angry, just confused.

'Why?' I asked, my mouth stumbling through the sounds.

'I'm sorry, Lia,' she said. 'We can't afford it.'

My mum always used the word 'we' in these kinds of conversations. She was clever like that. She made it very hard to argue. She made it very hard to be selfish.

'But—'

'I know how important this is to you,' she said. 'It's important to me too.' And then she sat down beside me, and extended a long arm around my waist, and pulled me to her, so I could rest my head on her shoulder, soft but solid, smelling of citrus and rosemary.

I wanted to be angry; a crescendo had started to build. But I knew I couldn't be. Instead, I tried to swallow the sobs that were emerging like the lone beats of a snare drum. I didn't want her to feel any worse than she already did.

The funny thing was that my piano lessons never actually stopped. My piano teacher, a kindly woman in her sixties who I liked to imagine had been a hippy at some time or other, kept coming.

When September came, Mum said she was staying home rather than going to Venice with a friend – a trip she'd been looking forward to, dreaming of, for years, after decades of not going back to Italy – and so I didn't have to go stay with 'Auntie' Maggie after all. I was surprised and asked why.

'Oh, Cathy had a work emergency, so she had to cancel, and I didn't want to go on my own,' she said, shrugging and returning to her crochet.

'But you were so desperate to see the Rialto Bridge! And don't you always say that English Italian food tastes nothing like the real thing?'

'I'll go in a few years,' was all she said, not looking up. But the years passed, and she never did.

In hindsight I wonder if she was avoiding my gaze.

The doctor's waiting room is both chaotic and languid. People in the queue huff. Children fidget. Everyone's staring off into space, wondering when their turn will come. Phones ring in the background, unanswered. *This is a land beyond time*, I think to myself. That reminds me of *The Land Before Time*, and dinosaurs. Dinosaur eggs. I haven't got a T-Rex hibernating in my living room, have I? Surely a T-Rex egg would be bigger?

Look at me, trying to apply logic to the situation.

I get up from my thinly padded chair and walk over to the water fountain, take a too-small paper cone and fill it, sending bubbles up through the cooler. I fill it again, and return to my seat, abdomen twinging as I soothe my dry mouth.

Finally they call my name. I stand up, and then wonder whether to run for it. What am I going to say to the doctor, after all? It was madness to come here – even madder than thinking you've laid an egg.

It's too late, anyway. The lady that takes people to their appointments has seen the whites of my eyes. I can't leave now. I drag my feet towards the door at the corner of the waiting room, attempt feebly to return her kindly smile. Her brow furrows. She must think something's really wrong with me. I wonder if she can sense it, with each patient she calls – this one diabetes, this one a migraine, this one irritable bowel. For a moment I wish she were a seer, putting her hand to my forehead as if to take my temperature, eyes rolling in her head as she tells me what it is that will burst forth from a cracked shell in my living room any day now. I kneel at her feet, kissing them in thanks. The relief of knowing, for better or for worse.

But she gestures down the corridor, tells me to go to room three, and then she and her clipboard are gone.

I knock, take a deep breath, steel myself.

'Come in.'

It's a male doctor, as I imagined. White-blond hair, pale skin, eyebrows barely there. Not too much older than me, which makes me nervous. Eyes anthracite-grey and oddly captivating, so that I can't look away. For some reason I notice how white and freckled his arms are, how the translucent hairs stand almost on end. It's cold in the room; I don't understand why he doesn't put on a jumper, or long sleeves. Perhaps he isn't allowed. I wish I'd asked for a woman, but I was too embarrassed to admit my embarrassment. And now I have to tell him what's wrong with me, and just hope he doesn't need to do any poking around.

He smiles. 'Make yourself comfortable. Have you come far?' he asks, trying to put me at ease. But as soon as he's hammered a few things into his keyboard – bringing up my records, no doubt – it's all business.

'Date of birth?'

I confirm.

'Taking any medication?

'Suffering any shortness of breath, dizziness?

'Any family history of heart disease, diabetes or high blood pressure?'

I hesitate, explain about the half that's unknown. It's practical to mention at times like this.

'Do you plan to have children?'

From staring at the floor, my head jerks up to look at him.

'What?' I blurt, before I can take it back or make it sound more polite.

'Do you plan to have children?'

My mind is racing. I'm remembering bending double over the toilet seat, shivering, wanting to vomit. I suddenly have the urge to ask the doctor whether he thinks I should, an aching for him to tell me The Answer, take the decision out of my hands. He looks wise. Maybe he's the seer. Maybe he knows some secret only doctors know. Maybe he'll be an Oscar Wilde, master of the pithy maxim that becomes a motto to live by.

This is not a land beyond time at all. Time reaches here too; the place is ready to burst with it. All it needs is for the doctor to press a red button and speed the whole thing up.

Something twinges near my left hip bone. *Do you plan to have children?*

'Why do you ask?'

'At your age, it's worth thinking about. You're almost a geriatric mother. Medical advice – do it earlier if you can.'

He says this all extremely matter-of-factly, reeling off a prescription. I think of all the women I know who've had children into their forties. 'That's not—'

I want to say, *That's not why I'm here*, but then I think of the egg. Or, *That's not what I meant*, but then how to explain?

'I'm feeling these strange pains.'

No mention of the egg, of course. Now that I'm here, I see how ridiculous it was to ever think that I could say it. The words simply don't go together, and once released into the room they'd only career into each other, leave destruction in their wake. This doctor, with his grey eyes, blue plastic scrubs and half-chewed biro, would never understand. He's used to spreadsheets and graphs and syringes wrapped in plastic. Even if this has happened before, to other women, he wouldn't know it. He wouldn't know it if he saw it with his own eyes.

'Tell me more about the pains,' he says, and as I talk he types, fingers flying over the keyboard, hammering away, eyes flickering from screen to keyboard to me to keyboard to screen.

The question I most want answered curls tighter around my stomach, unasked. An arrow of pain. I bite my tongue. The egg will still be there when I get home. Biding its time.

Last month, in the office. Strip lighting and open-plan desks. The clear desk policy respected by no one. 'Pentatonic' in stodgy purple text across the wall, in case we've forgotten where we work. In Production, they get purple music notes too, vinyls in black frames and signed photographs on the walls. I can only dream of being upgraded to that one day. No need for that in Corporate. Aside from some lacklustre Christmas decorations, Post-its provided the only other flashes of colour: on computer screens, on divider walls, on the backs of seats reserved for people in need of lumbar support.

My colleague had brought in a baby. Well, not just any baby – not a baby she'd found somewhere by the wayside and decided to borrow for the day. Her baby. She'd been off for two months, on maternity leave. And somehow, between disappearing with a bump the size of a carry-on suitcase and stopping by the office that day, she'd acquired a small human being.

It was time for show-and-tell.

People crowded round like birds at the watering hole. They drank the infant in with their eyes, thirsty for youth or good fortune or the impression of serenity for a few seconds. My colleague's smile was wide, but I could read the sleepless nights in her eyes. I looked a moment too long.

'Would you like to hold him?' she said, mistaking my fascination.

Immediately I felt ill-equipped. I didn't know how to place my arms, where to support the bundle she was thrusting in my direction. It felt like too great a responsibility. What if I did it wrong, caused irreversible damage, looked like an idiot? What if he burped up on me?

'Look at him. He likes you,' my colleague cooed. Now the crowd was around me, except they weren't, of course – they were around the baby. He was heavier and warmer than I'd expected. His pale lentil eyelids had closed, pink and veiny. His soft forehead was almost translucent. He lay still, at peace. I looked down at him, pictured him mine. Pictured nursing this little creature, being with him at my waking and my sleeping. I was vaguely aware that I was supposed to feel something. I imagined my heart being tugged downwards, as if pulled on sinewy strings by his tiny, clenched fists. His warmth spread through my body, and I felt a protectiveness. He was pretty, it's true. But no tug, and the twinge in my ovaries was only the pain I'd been feeling for months, making me wonder how long I'd have to wait for my follow-up at the doctor's.

Or perhaps, rather than with Safa, *that* was the moment the egg began to form, the shell forming sharp as crystal, stabbing at my insides.

The baby opened his eyes and started to scrunch up his face, wave his fists from side to side and kick. Suddenly he was writhing like a reptile, and I was terrified I'd drop him. I braced myself for him to wail, rushing over to his mother who was chatting to someone just a few metres away, reaching out hurriedly to hand him over. My colleague chuckled wearily. 'He's easier when he's sleeping, isn't he?'

His weight and warmth were gone. I could breathe again. I made for the stairs, took myself outside to the fresh air and the open sky and decided to go for a walk. Unburdened, I roamed free, and my head filled with music, black-and-white notes dancing through my vision, snakes and ladders up and down a scale.

I sit at the keyboard in my music room, troubled by the depth of my pain. It feels as if someone's tugging hard on my womb from the inside. I press one of the white keys, smooth and cool as bone. A rich note vibrates through the air. Slowly every part of me awakens, from the hairs on my arm to the chambers of my heart to the nuclei of my cells. First, they tremble. And then they dance. And then everything, my pain and the egg included, ripples and melts away.

My phone buzzes. It's my friend Dimitri. 'We need to meet. The usual place.' It's Friday night, a week since the egg arrived. He and his partner brought home their own bundle of joy six weeks ago. He's been sending me pictures of Hannah every few days: in her Babygro, in the bath, lying on her play mat, asleep in bed with Dimitri's partner, Omar. But every time I've sent him actual words in return, I've got nothing back. My questions have been left unanswered. I know he's busy, but about a week ago I started to wonder whether maybe the photos weren't only for me: maybe they were a mass message, a broadcast. At least on Instagram you know you're not special.

I'd like to send him pictures of the egg: me with the egg on the sofa, me with the egg obscuring my face. I wonder if then he would reply.

I finish work and leave the egg, finding it easier to do so the longer it goes without hatching. I'm starting to wonder if it will simply become part of the furniture, a sort of constant question mark that I'll never quite escape. I arrive at our pub with my defences up, still a little hurt by the idea that Dimitri wasn't thinking specifically of me. But I can't help feeling relieved when I see him.

I expected him to look different somehow. Aged, from all the sleepless nights. Or more wrinkled, a sign of his increasing wisdom. Or bioluminescent, perhaps, glowing with the sweetest, most magical love anyone could ever know.

Instead, he's the same old Dimitri. Round-faced and clean-shaven, short dark hair, skin brown as the olive bark of his native Greece. He's wearing a plain black T-shirt, like always (despite the chill) and distressed jeans with the kind of shredded knees that only money can buy. He seems too relaxed for this pub, which is bustling with office workers desperate to let off steam, a grumpy queue at the bar and bartenders with octopus arms.

We used to meet here almost every week, ever since we volunteered at the youth club together. But not since Hannah was born. To be fair, I hesitated to leave the egg at home. But it doesn't need feeding or changing, and nor does it fit in my handbag.

'Sit down, sit down!' he gestures impatiently as I approach the corner table he's chosen. 'We need to talk.'

It seems I'm not even allowed to go get a drink, but I don't mind. This is the Dimitri I know. I start to smile, then suppress it. I know it's hard when you have a baby, but he could have responded to at least one of my messages.

'I'm sorry I haven't got back to you, Lia. I feel awful!' he says, as if he's read my mind. 'You can't imagine how busy we've been – we've barely had a minute to think. All I manage to do is send those pictures to you and my brother, and then I feel so terrible every time you reply and I don't reply back. I've been meaning to; I promise you I have. And I've been reading them. And' – here he takes my hand in his and makes a point of looking me in the eye – 'I've appreciated them.'

The messages were personal, after all. Everything is forgiven. How could it not be? Finally, I allow myself to smile.

'So how have you been?' I ask.

He throws his hands in the air, slumps back against the cushioned wall. 'You know what? If I have to change another nappy I think I'm going to murder someone.'

My face must have twisted in concern because he follows it up hastily with, 'But it's worth it. Honestly, it is worth it. When I hold Hannah…' And then he goes all dreamy, to that state I've seen in others before, a kind of faraway land I don't know if I'll ever find.

'Listen,' he says, and grabs my hand again. 'What can I get you to drink? I didn't come here to talk about babies. I came here to talk about anything but. A G&T? Let me get you one, and then you can tell me everything.' He gives me a big hug and scoots out from under the table to go to the bar. The hug lingers while he's there, and so does my smile.

And when he gets back, I start to tell him everything. Not about the egg, of course. So I hold back quite a big something. But I tell him the rest.

I talk about how I'm still hoping to get put on something more exciting at work, something actually related to music.

I tell him about Mum's prognosis. About my pains. And about my feeling that time is running out on the baby decision. And he listens. And he doesn't tell me what to do.

'Look, Omar and I, we're over the moon. But we knew what we wanted. You – you need to get away from it all. Ignore the voices around you. Where's David at the moment, anyway?'

'He's away,' I say, thinking of Whitstable, thinking that I owe David an answer.

'Perfect. So, it's just you and the egg,' he says.

I splutter on my gin, heart pounding, eyelids throbbing. Trying to process what he's just said. How does he know? Not a soul has seen the egg but me; unless… I think of *The Truman Show*, of the horror films with the unsuspecting protagonist – everyone's in on it except her, everyone around her is slowly laying a trap, and nothing is what it seems.

Suddenly the room is zooming in and out, my heart inflating and deflating with it – everything is too loud – stools screech like train brakes – the air is stifling, too full of other people's breath – the laughter from the bar grates, clamouring in my ears, blocking out my thoughts. Maybe this isn't Dimitri at all but some kind of avatar; I look to see if his teeth are pointed or there are circuit boards flashing in his irises, or maybe this whole thing is a dream, reality fraying at the edges.

I clutch at the table edge, trying to steady myself. There's a clanging coming from somewhere, constant, inescapable.

'Are you OK?' the creature says, reaching its hand out to me. I recoil, still trying to work out if I've entered a nightmare.

'What did you say?' I manage to get out, my voice wavering.

'It's just you and your head,' he says simply.

Back to earth. Dimitri looks normal again: flesh and blood and denim. The clanging stops. The pub crowd chatters on in the background at a comfortable volume, just loud enough to make a conversation effortful.

'You're a good friend, Dimitri,' I say weakly, my heart only beginning to slow, taking a deep breath and pressing my feet into the ground, letting him take my hand in his.

'Well, you'll have to meet Hannah soon,' he says, and takes another sip of his lager.

'That would be lovely,' I say, and I mean it. My breathing returns to normal. I settle into the evening once more. But then:

'Right, I've got to go,' he says, plonking his glass in the centre of the table and shuffling for his coat. 'It was so special to see you,' he says.

I deflate a little; this time because it's as if he's waved his hand in front of my mouth and snatched a handful of air just before I could breathe it in.

He's right. These seventy-two minutes have been special. But what's 'special' and 'normal' have been turned inside out.

For a moment I consider sending Meg of the 3 a.m. dancing a message. '*Bit last minute – are you around?*' But the thought of the egg stops me.

As we leave our pub together, the men have taken off their ties and the women are swapping their heels for flats, as they order another round.

Mum is worse: the debris of used mugs and cutlery piled around her has grown, and her plants are beginning to look neglected. She seems so tired even smiling to say hello is an effort, but she does, and I'm grateful. Grateful that she's still here.

As her eyes crinkle I wonder if she always had so many crows' feet. If I'll ever have that many. Somehow her irises are still lustrous and blue as sapphire, even when the rest of her has greyed. Her hands are so frail they look ready to crumble into ash; her once jet hair grey, and so thin it's already dust. She's in her usual chair, wrapped in her Nonna blanket, the one her grandmother crocheted in Sicily before my grandmother took it to Rome and then wrapped my mother in it when she was wriggling in her cot. Its bright colours make me think of limoncello and oranges, raw red prawns and sparkling surf. Once again, the clutter of photo frames fills me with the urge to ask about these women who came before me, their men, their children. I want to know what their lives were composed of, as if that is something anyone can ever tell you, as if a life were a perfectly formed hazelnut, shiny and smooth and easy to hold in the palm of your hand. I want to write songs about them, even knowing that a song could only ever sum up one tiny aspect of the million and one aspects of a person's existence.

She speaks slowly, as if dredging for energy, but the more she speaks the more energy she seems to find, and so I keep asking my questions.

She tells me of the day my grandmother Chiara decided to leave Sicily for Rome: 'She booked her crossing that very same day, with the meagre items she'd been saving for her trousseau, and got home and packed her bags, even though she wasn't leaving for three and a half weeks!' she says, spluttering with laughter, and I can picture Nonna Chiara telling her the story herself, a mischievous smile on her face. I dare not interrupt, lest she pull back from the anecdote like she so often does when she speaks about her mother. 'She used to tell me that even before she arrived in Rome, she knew her way around the city as well as she knew how to walk the streets of her village without leaving the shade. And it was true – everywhere we went she'd point out locations from the movies. I used to ask her where she'd like to be filmed one day.'

She tells me the story of my grandparents' wedding, blue hyacinths and cannoli pastries, my grandmother and grandfather kissing beside the Tiber. 'My childhood was a happy one, at least in the beginning.' And I want to ask more, but don't feel I can, the rest of that story contained in another volume, on a cobwebbed shelf too high to reach.

'It was always your nonno who did the cooking,' she says, smiling with her tongue curled around her teeth, as if she can taste his marinara. 'And he would organise great escapades for us, excursions to the coast in a rattling Cinquecento, a carefully packed picnic of prosciutto, crusty bread and, in May, green almonds. He taught me how to extract them from the fuzzy green flesh, and then to twist my arm back and throw the skins as far as I could into the sea. That was when we would visit his sister, your great aunt Antonella.' Here she pauses, as if unsure whether to go on. 'Your grandmother loved those trips too. She loved to wear her hair tied up in a scarf, and she loved it when he said she looked like Marilyn Monroe.'

I realise, listening to my mother, that just as I don't know enough about the stories behind these photos, I don't know what her life is really composed of either. For me, it is as if she has had two lives: the first, with her own unanswered questions, of who to love, what to strive for, of benefits of hindsight and no-undoing-the-clock, where she grew up in a suburb of Rome, met my father one dolce-vita night — a sun-braised Sicilian sailor, or at least that's what he said, who spoke like her mamma — and then never heard from him again. And then this life, the one which belongs to me, in which she's a mother, in which she has left her country and her language behind, and come to this city to start again, and settled, and looked after me, and I've long assumed her questions were all answered.

But now it occurs to me that there is a third life too, a life I've rarely thought about, the one happening in secret, behind the second life, where still she asks herself *Am I fulfilled?* and *Have I done enough?* and misses those who are no longer here, and may or may not wish there were someone in bed beside her, and fills her quiet hours when I'm not around, and thinks about self-improvement, and, lately, thinks about entering a cave where all is still, and quiet and cool, but perhaps a bit clammy, and the lights have gone out.

I wish there were space to sit next to her in the armchair, to huddle together under the Nonna blanket, to synchronise my breath with hers like I used to as a child.

Instead I stay on the sofa. I ask her to tell her own stories:

'Why did you leave Italy?' And, 'Where did you meet my father?'

(I don't ask about the rest, there's no need, I know she's already said all there is to say, and I already know all I need to know) and how she left, while still pregnant with me, and came to London and found a home – this house, that we're sitting in now – of why she called me Lia (she's told me before, it means 'bringer of good news'), and whether she ever feels alone.

'I've always known how to look after myself. Until now, anyway,' she smiles weakly. 'That's not to say there's never been anyone in my life. But I know what it's like to have someone who comes and goes. I couldn't do that to you.'

'Do you mean Nonna?' I ask. But as is so often the case when I try to understand how things came to be broken, she doesn't respond.

I wish I had a pen and paper; my head is so full of her stories I'm worried they might leak away, rivers flowing out into the room and away on the ether, irretrievable when I want them again.

And I wonder who I'll tell these stories to, who they will matter to. I can see my friends' eyes glazing over as I recount the minutiae. Even David will only listen for a while, before his interest fades. It needs someone who feels something stirring deep within them as these stories unfold, who feels the tug of sinew across the space-time continuum, connecting them, deep in their DNA, to their share in these stories, as the hazelnut is polished again and again, made more perfect each time, until it shines.

These are stories to tell your grandchildren.

⊙

At home, I sit by the egg again. What else?

It's still silent, of course, but suddenly I see something different when I look at it.

Possibility.

I make myself a cup of tea, cradle it in my hands, sitting cross-legged by the nest. For some reason I talk to it – telling it the stories my mother has told me.

'Can you hear me?' I ask. I sing the lullaby my mother used to sing: '*Fa la ninna, fa la nanna…*' I sing 'Beyond You'.

I get up, ignoring a twinge in my lower back, and find more towels and a blanket I've had since childhood. I build the nest higher and thicker. I stroke the egg, cupping my hand to match its curves.

'When do I get to meet you?' I ask out loud. I've been speaking to the egg more and more; does this count as talking to myself? There's so much more I want to say, but it's hard to tell if anything's listening.

'David will be back soon,' I reassure it, giving it a pat, craving his presence as much as I'm nervous about picking up where we left off.

It doesn't respond.

Of course it doesn't. It's an egg.

I met her once. I was six. We went to the zoo. I remember her peroxide hair, how it was almost as white as her fluffy coat. Her eyes were black as ash and made me think of Etna, the live volcano we'd studied at school. She smiled down at me with dark plum lips, striking against her olive skin, and I thought she was the most beautiful woman I'd ever seen. After some rummaging in a brown snakeskin handbag, she extracted some sweets wrapped in brightly coloured paper and knelt down to hold them out to me. 'Almond cookies,' she said, and when she smiled so close to me I saw that all her teeth were perfect.

I didn't understand why Mum stood so stiffly when Nonna hugged her, nor why she stepped away so quickly. 'Let's go,' she said sternly, and jerked my hand, marching away from Regent's Park station with my grandmother hurrying to keep up, her red patent kitten heels tapping out a rushed rhythm on the pavement.

Nonna spoke to my mother in something like Italian which I couldn't understand, while the three of us stood behind glass, watching the monkeys pick fleas off each other. She spoke tentatively, perhaps asking a question. When my mum replied I remember thinking she sounded so *tired*, which was odd because it was well before bedtime. I had the impression she was explaining something, and then her tone sharpened, and I snapped my head round to see anger flashing in her eyes.

'Come, Lia,' Mum said.

The rest of the afternoon continued liked that: Mum marching off, dragging me along with her; Nonna catching up a minute or two after we reached each enclosure, looking out of place each time I twisted round to see if she was keeping up, weaving in and out of parents and children in her white fluffy coat and red kitten heels.

I was terrified of saying even a word to her; I didn't understand why my mother was so angry, but I was worried that if I said anything at all, Mum would make us leave the zoo immediately – or worse, send my grandmother away.

Finally, we were gifted a few minutes alone. We came out of the reptile house, where I'd had a mad urge to grab Nonna's handbag and hide it under my coat lest the snakes see it and be struck down with sorrow – or worse, rage that would send them smashing through their tanks towards us, fangs bared.

We scrunched our faces and squinted as the sunlight overcame us, and I remember seeing a pregnant woman and thinking, *This must be what it's like to come out of the womb into the world for the first time.* I understood why babies cried so much.

My mother announced that she needed the ladies'. I knew this to be a trait of hers: that she would go to the toilet more frequently than I was physically capable of, and do so immediately after making her intentions known. It was only when we were both older, when she became more familiar with doctors and hospitals, that we understood.

My mother's eyes darted from sign to sign. My nonna caught my eye and winked, as if we were in on a secret.

'This way!' my mother declared, and tried to take my hand, but I whipped it away. 'Lia, let's go,' she said, firm but impatient.

'I don't need to!' I replied, folding my arms so that she couldn't grab my hand.

'Just come with me, Lia,' she said, and I could tell she was annoyed, because her eyes narrowed the way they did when I wouldn't get in the bath.

'Won't. I went before the reptile house!' I retorted.

She looked at me. She looked at my nonna. She looked at me again.

'*Mannaggia!*' she said, and walked in the straightest line possible to the hut where the toilets were.

I turned to my nonna, beaming. She bent down and pinched my cheek, the way I'd seen them do in the movies.

'You're a clever girl, Lia,' she said, her Italian vowels nasal and curt. 'And I'm very pleased to meet you.'

'I can speak Sicilian!' I said, full of pride.

'Oh?'

I sang her the first line of my mother's lullaby: '*Fa la ninna, fa la nanna…*' Her plum lips began to move, and soon she was singing along too.

When my mother returned from the toilet I thought she'd be angry, but she wasn't. In fact, she even smiled, water gathering at the corner of her eyes.

Monday, and I'm supposed to be working: there are timelines to be met, suppliers to contact. Instead I'm in the living room staring at the egg and scouring the web, trying to find out if this has ever happened to anyone before. Perhaps not with an egg. Perhaps with an animal, like the Victorian rabbit lady. Or even some inanimate object, like a stone.

Perhaps I should message Jess. Jess would know.

I find an article explaining why hens lay eggs even without roosters. Eggs that will never develop or hatch into a chick. The article notes that some hens will never lay eggs at all, either due to poor diet or, more often, a genetic defect.

The first eggs laid may have soft shells or abnormal shapes, it says. *Contact your veterinarian if one of your hens seems to be having trouble.* There are tips for how to tell if a freshly laid egg is fertilised, whether there's anything inside. You're supposed to hold it up to the light, check for 'shape and opacity' and 'blood spots'.

I look at the egg again. Shape: oval. Opacity: opaque. Blood spots: not evident.

I find another article, about a lizard in Australia that is evolving before zoologists' eyes, transitioning from egg-laying to 'giving live birth'. It says animals that lay eggs are 'oviparous'. Good to know what they'll write on my tombstone, at least. But it also says that egg-laying developed first. *Many physiological changes were necessary for live birth to evolve.* I'm the first ever example of backward evolution.

I stare at the photo of the three-toed skink, my nose getting closer and closer to the screen. It's like a brown slithering slow-worm with tiny legs surely too fragile to be of any use. I pinch with my fingers, zoom in some more. I try to see if I can feel any affinity with its beady brown eye.

I search one more time. And finally, I find it. A Norwegian farmer's wife who laid an egg in 1639. A mother of twelve. *Pious, otherwise completely unremarkable*, the article says. Twelve children: *unremarkable*! Records suggest she had been ill for a year before the laying, suffering from weakness and vertigo. It took an entire day.

An expert in unusual phenomena declared the Devil had exchanged the woman's unborn child for an egg. And then he kept the egg in his private collection for the rest of his life.

I accompany Mum to the clinic and she excuses herself to use the loo halfway through, shuffling to the door – refusing my offer of assistance – and leaving me with her doctor, a kindly middle-aged woman with a neatly trimmed, greying Afro and a soft but weary bedside manner.

I find myself wondering why all doctors' offices have the same kind of blinds – those long strips that hang vertically, threaded together with strings of plastic beads. I'm reminded of Mum's old rosary; my thoughts circle in on themselves as if fingering first this bead, then the next, before returning to the first again, my eyes drawn to the geometric floor tiles which spiral so that I can't work out where the pattern begins or ends.

Doctor Abioye has just told us that Mum only has a year or two left.

I'm counting the prayer beads in my head, trying to focus on the here and now. We've always known this disease would get her eventually, but I didn't think it would happen so soon.

The chair is uncomfortable – hard plastic, no cushioning. I wonder how long Mum will be in the loo.

'Maybe the two of us should talk for a moment,' the doctor says.

I'm suddenly conscious of my heartbeat as I brace myself for what she might say.

'You care for your mother, don't you?'

For a moment I'm blank. 'Of course, I love her loads.'

There's a pause. Doctor Abioye looks at me as if I'm stupid, brow furrowed. 'I meant—'

'Ah. Yes. No. Sort of. She has a few friends that visit too, help her with cleaning, things like that. I do pop round a lot, if that's what you mean.' *In between incubating my egg, going to work, shopping for my neighbour Mary and going to the soup kitchen*, I think, *but I haven't had much time for that lately*.

'You may need to pop round a bit more often.'

Tick.

She pauses, pursing already-thin lips, and furrowing an already-furrowed brow. 'Look, your mother is strong. But things are going to get difficult for her over the next few months. She's going to need you a lot. You might want to consider moving in with her or finding someone who can look after her full time.'

My prayer beads unravel and scatter across the floor, chaos versus tessellated order.

'The next few... months?' I splutter, barely able to get the words out, barely able to compute.

'I'm sorry – I didn't mean to scare you. Like I told you both, she should have longer than that. A few years, maybe more, though I know that's still difficult to hear. She's a fighter, I can see that. But as I explained, she's going to change more quickly than we thought.'

Change. What a strange euphemism. I think of caterpillars becoming butterflies. I think of the wind blowing south, then north by north-west. I think of autumn leaves turning.

I take a deep breath.

'What should I expect?'

Tock.

Now, when I see pregnant women, I think that they have dinosaur eggs tied to their stomachs, beneath their clothes, like little girls shoving pillows under their T-shirts.

I take the Tube after work, rattling to and fro as we burrow deeper into central London, until eventually I emerge on to the artificial glow of Oxford Street, a blur of people in all shapes, sizes and shades. I want to buy a gift for Safa's baby, for when it comes. I'll look at Hamleys first, though Regent Street isn't really the place for a Junior Project Manager to shop. Mercifully it's a little quieter there, too. A form of natural selection, I think sardonically.

My phone buzzes in my pocket, just about audible beneath the rumbling traffic. I stop, take it out, get shouted at by a man trying to rush past me. It's the hospital I've been referred to, confirming my appointment for my next test, to find out what's wrong with me – cancer, cysts, endometriosis, it's-all-in-my-head – the possibilities swirling like the crowds that weave in and out of each other on the pavement. I look up and see a woman stooped over, trying to pick up a dropped glove; she's round, enormous, must be at least eight months, her egg-shaped belly a hindrance to reaching the ground.

'Here,' I say, bending easily to snatch it up and hand it to her, the Greek-style columns of a men's suit shop towering behind her.

She looks back at me, black irises in white eyes surrounded by dark skin. 'Thanks,' she says, and her cheeks dimple. She's close enough in age to be one of my friends, another Safa. Another one saying goodbye to youth and taking the plunge into Real Adulthood. As she walks past me, I try to picture myself weighed down like that, waddling, maybe curling my hands protectively around my belly. Imagine my skin pulled taut over something growing bigger each day. Carrying a living thing inside me, a precious cargo or a parasite, depending on how you look at it, sitting still, trying to sense its heartbeat, crying out with joy and surprise every time I feel a kick.

I pause, look down at my own stomach, get jostled and told off again. Impossible to imagine my body should ever look that way, impossible to imagine I could ever carry something like that around; even despite the egg, I feel it's not what I was made for, though I know it is; I feel it wouldn't be right; this woman I've helped must be a different kind of human, another sex – or perhaps I am, and I just can't see it the same way others do.

In the immortal words of my secondary-school biology teacher: it's like trying to crap a watermelon.

Maybe if foetuses could be left to develop at home, wrapped in a nest of towels, beside the radiator. Maybe then.

But when I get home and I see the egg sitting in its nest by the radiator, its blankness affronts me. No longer merely mysterious, nearly two weeks of waiting have made it threatening. There could be anything in there. Anything. With horror I imagine it hatching; blood, gore, and what else might emerge? A tiny version of myself, mutilated, perhaps, a Dorian Gray of my soul? What if it's dangerous – a bloodsucking creature that leaps for me, fangs bared, devouring its creator, and leaving her a pile of bones on the living room floor, like the sad remains of a hastily scoffed KFC family bucket? What if it's a Satanic spirit, or Beelzebub himself, unleashed upon the world by an unsuspecting girl in Sydenham? I've seen the films; I know how these things start, and I know how they end…

It could be something nice. It could be a beautiful little chick, fluffy and soft, which I could nuzzle and hold and show to David and my friends with pride. Perhaps it'll be a creature no one's ever heard of, like an elongated, rainbow-coloured cat, amphibious (as it's from an egg), with magical powers to help me in my everyday life. Maybe it'll be a friend to me in difficult times, snuggle with me in bed in the mornings, infuse me with its warmth, sing with me, cure me of all my ills.

But even this image doesn't ring true. Whatever it is will need looking after. Whatever it is, I will have to keep secret. I imagine being tethered to this house, having to come back early every night to look after my Thing, feeding it – the expense! – worrying about it, whether it's OK and what it's getting up to. I see my music room gathering dust, my songwriter dreams forgotten. My breath starts to catch in my throat, my heart to quiver.

None of this makes sense. But then, nor does the egg.

Suddenly filled with purpose, I stand up with a force that surprises me; I don't even need to use my hands. I look around the room, at photo frames, messily piled books, souvenirs from weekends away with David, haphazardly placed cushions, dirty mugs. I need something heavy, and maybe sharp, and big. I don't want to just crack this thing – that risks a halfway house, time for regret, maybe discovering what's in there and wishing I hadn't done it, scrambling to save it, and then realising it's too late.

I need to obliterate it in one go.

I rush to the kitchen. On the side, drying, a cast-iron casserole dish. I lift it, gritting my teeth, my core once again screaming in protest, even though I thought I'd recovered.

Back in the living room I stand, lifting it above my head, surprised how much I have to heave, amazed by its weight. I look down at the egg, ready to drop the dish, ready and accepting of whatever destruction will follow. My breath is heavy and quick now, desperate gasps for air, trying to catch up with my own adrenaline.

The egg stares back up at me, blank as ever.

I have to know.

My arms start to burn. The casserole feels heavier and heavier by the second.

I look down at the egg, willing myself to do it.

I wonder if whatever's inside will crunch like twigs or snap like a wishbone.

One simple motion. One release.

Still nothing happens. Still I do nothing.

Slowly, I lower the dish, place it on the coffee table with a clang.

Exhausted, I almost collapse, folding my legs underneath me, leaning over the egg and curling up around it. Helpless.

Gradually, I drift off, into a slumber filled with fire-breathing dragons, haggard versions of myself and long purple cats with neat rows of pointed, deadly fangs.

I'm trying to talk to Mum, but instead of words the only thing coming from her mouth is a chirping. It's distant and regular, like the backing track to a country walk. I'm worried, want to understand what she's trying to say. She's been getting worse.

'How are you feeling?' I ask again, but though she moves her mouth as if to form syllables, only birdsong emerges.

'I can't understand you,' I say, my eyes brimming with tears. If I can't understand, I can't help. I do so want to help.

And still this birdsong.

Suddenly I'm awake and light is creeping around the curtains. I'm still lying draped over the egg, back aching from my awkward position. There's a chirping, but it's coming from inside the egg. I scrunch up my eyes and try to go back to the dream. But then I feel a tap from inside the eggshell, right under my left hand, and jump back in surprise. I stand up, look down at this impossible object wrapped in its towels. More chirping. A rat-a-tat-tat. And then on one side of the egg a small crack starts to appear.

HATCHING

When I was thirteen, school took us to see a Uruguayan pianist. I didn't go away thinking I wanted to be Beethoven, but I did start wearing star-shaped glasses and singing 'Goodbye Yellow Brick Road' until Mum said she couldn't bear to listen to it any more.

After a sick-making coach ride where the class sang an atonal rendition of 'Green Bottles' and someone managed to block the toilet five minutes into the journey, we pulled up outside a concrete concert hall straight from a dystopia. Our teacher told us it had won architecture awards in its time, but it only made us feel small, and we shuffled with trepidation through the revolving glass doors.

Once inside there was one commotion after another to check our tickets, fight our way through the other school groups and find our seats. Finally, everything was in place.

The auditorium went dark. A spotlight roved across the stage. A man with slumped shoulders and a weakly knotted tie shuffled to the piano stool.

He sat down at the great instrument. He extended a hand. A single note rang out across the hall, pure and unfiltered. There was a titter from somewhere near the back. It was always from the back, at this age.

But he didn't seem to notice, and before anyone could shift their weight in their seat, he was throwing himself into it heart and soul, fingers leaping across the keys, his suddenly assertive torso writhing, twisting and diving to keep up. Now not a soul was moving, perhaps even breathing. It was less a tune and more a trip, jerking from one thing to the next when you least expected it.

'Bit mental,' Safa whispered next to me, grinning broadly, cheeks dimpled, unable to do anything but feel impressed. She hadn't yet discovered kohl and lipstick, but she didn't need to. She was already pretty enough for half the boys (and some of the girls) in school to be after her, and all the girls to envy her.

But after an initial hush, as the piece went on there were a couple of coughs. I saw a few students in front whisper to a neighbour. A girl to my left started redoing her ponytail.

I didn't understand how people could do this. I was transfixed; I forgot everything. His energy was my energy, his concentration was my concentration, and I was up there with him, finding the keys, applying exactly the right amount of pressure, and ending with a flourish.

Ending. I couldn't believe it was over. I felt winded, lost. I was brought back to my seat, and suddenly the room looked tawdry, the students around me tatty and rude.

'Well, he was great!' Safa said, but she was already leaning to offer someone behind her a gummy sweet. She was already moving on to the next thing, before I'd even finished applauding. Before the pianist had even left the stage.

On the coach on the way home I asked Safa if she'd ever be a pianist. She thought for a moment, sucking on her sweet.

'Musician, maybe,' she said. 'But in a band. Don't you think he looked a bit lonely?'

'He was alone up there,' I said by way of an answer. 'But that's not the same.'

I'm holding my breath, Pandora with her hand on the lid, expecting everything to happen all at once: the shell to collapse in on itself, and whatever's in there to emerge victorious, cawing or breathing fire or whatever else it might do. But instead, the process unfolds gradually, giving time for the weight in my stomach to grow heavier and heavier, braced for fangs and talons.

After a first small hole takes shape, all I hear for a while is a tapping. I want to kneel next to the egg, try to peer in through the jagged hole and see what's happening, but fear keeps me taut. Slowly, more cracks form around the hole, fault lines in the desert. The tip of a beak begins to surface, black and pointed, a blunt dagger. My jaw is clenched, my hands fists. I feel nauseous. There's a strange smell in the air, of something warm and only half-formed. Gradually, the rest of its head becomes visible, no bigger than a date.

You can't undo something like this.

I had my moment to flush, and I didn't take it. This is now a blood pact, no going back.

Whatever it is, it's covered in feathers, bedraggled and gooey. I think of under-fried eggs, the white wobbly and glistening. The hole becomes a crevasse, the shell shifting tectonically around it. Eventually, I can see the beginnings of a body.

It's a bird.

I'm frozen, looking down at this creature that shouldn't be here and yet somehow is. Its eyes are clamped shut, so it's chipping blindly at the crack it has already made, slowly finding its way out of its prison. Larger pieces of shell fall away, as shoulders follow the head, a walnut-shaped body with folded wings and tail feathers streamlined for flight.

It's much smaller than I'd expected, much smaller than the egg, which is a relief. It's about the size of a sparrow, hunched over leathery pink feet with long ribbed toes. The saw-toothed remains of the egg lie around it in disarray.

And then it chirps and opens its beak wide, a gaping pink hole.

I look upon my unholy spawn.

It needs food.

I stand transfixed, praying this scene will go away.

'Wake up,' I mutter to myself, trying to break out of my trance, digging my fingernails into my palms.

I rush to the kitchen to see what I can find. I type *what do baby birds eat* into my phone, trying to focus on the task at hand rather than all the questions swirling through my head.

Baby birds eat what their parents eat for dinner. I look in the fridge. Leftover Chinese? I don't think so. Milk? Cheese?

Different birds eat different things. Still not helpful. If only David were here, he'd know what to do. No wonder he feels better equipped to deal with parenthood than me. I almost call him, then think better of it, then remember the time zones too.

At last: *worms, insects and seeds.* I look woefully at the phone screen, then open the cupboards again, ducking to avoid sharp edges tumbling out and catching me in the eye. I rummage, feeling my way to the back, past jars and half-sealed baggies and packets tied with elastic bands. Will my porridge chia seeds work? Bought in a health craze and barely touched. It's all I have. Scrolling through, I see other tips – moist dog food, boiled eggs (really? Surely cannibalism!), a 'no' to water, milk and baked goods. Later, I'll go to the shop. I hurry back to the living room.

Part of me wants the bird to look up at me, recognise me as its mother, call out. But with its eyes closed and its head waving around in all directions, it may not even know I'm here.

I crouch down next to it, both drawn to its downy head and repulsed by it. It still glistens with whatever gunk was inside the egg. It's small enough that it could easily sit in my cupped hands, but I'm about as keen for it to do that as if it were a cuck of leeches. I attempt to touch its cone-shaped head with the very tip of my finger, then draw my hand back as if from a burning stovetop, without even making contact. Finally I swallow my nausea and place the chia seeds in my hand, lie it flat and approach the bird's beak. 'Come on,' I try to say, in that ridiculous voice we use for creatures (and small humans) that can't understand us. My voice sounds strangled.

Immediately, the beak scrabbles at my palm. The pressure is a shock; the bird is really *here*, not mere delusion, though I wish it were.

It scrabbles some more, its beak oddly cold but sharp, a scalpel. I wince, withdraw my hand. It lets out a plaintive cry – whether searching for the food or its mother I don't know. It's apparent that method is not going to work. The next time the bird tilts its head back, I take my chance to drop the chia seeds directly into its moist, shining mouth. They are gratefully received; the chick gobbles and then chirps, gobbles and chirps, seemingly content. I watch all this as if a patient under local anaesthetic, seeing their guts being dissected right in front of their eyes.

'We'll be OK,' I say. And I try to believe it.

I call in sick for the remainder of the week. Bird is ravenous. No matter how much I feed her (I don't know if it's a 'her', but I've decided it is – projecting, probably) – chia, sunflower seeds, dead flies from my window ledge – she wants more, her cries growing louder and more insistent, so that I worry the neighbours will hear. Is this what Dimitri and Omar have been dealing with?

I wish David were here to help. I wish he were here to make it all better.

Bird's feathers have dried, and I can now look at her without shuddering. She doesn't move much, but stays mainly wrapped in her nest of towels, black-beetle eyes following the hand that feeds her.

I go to my keyboard, try to write, but my hands keep returning to the right-hand side of the piano and all I end up doing is attempting to replicate Bird's high-pitched trilling, playing the same notes in quick succession. The melody won't come, and when I look down at my page I see a single word: 'bird', again and again and again.

By the weekend, I start to think that it's time to tell David. The nightmare has progressed from inanimate object to living, breathing succubus. Until the egg hatched, I could tell myself that maybe it never would, that I could hide it away in the back of a cupboard or smash it with that casserole dish and get on with life with David as if nothing had happened. It's harder to do that with this feathered thing limping around spreading guano on the kitchen tiles.

It does cross my mind that there's still a way out. Abandonment, for one. Or passing her off as a bird I simply found somewhere and finding someone else to take her on.

Sing a song of sixpence, pocketful of rye... I picture the illustration in the book of nursery rhymes, the clawed feet poking out of the pastry, and shudder. I couldn't do that, could I?

I suppose there's a question of whether Bird has anything to do with David. David's never mentioned any unusual genes, but could she be his unholy spawn as well as mine? And if she is, does that mean I should tell him, give him the chance to be a feather father, perhaps even solo, if I decide to leave her behind? Is that what he'd want?

Perhaps I ought to tell him simply because we've always said No Secrets. Our relationship is uncodified; we haven't made any vows, but that doesn't stop the rules being there, unwritten, residing in convention, precedent and the principles of fair play.

Still, much as I repeat 'No Secrets' like a mantra, I've always been a little bit sceptical of it. Absolutism is rarely your friend. Surely we all have certain thoughts that are best kept to ourselves, emotions we may feel from time to time, fleeting or deeper rooted, where no benefit can be had from speaking their name? The people you find more attractive than your partner. The habits you can't stand but know there's no point trying to change. The pride you know too well not to wound.

Perhaps Bird fits in that category. A secret, yes, but a harmless one. Like a white lie *This Valentine's meal you've cooked is delicious. You're the best sex I've ever had.*

Or maybe she's the kind of secret that will fester and weep like a sore.

I spend my non-working hours (and some of my working hours) dashing back and forth from kitchen to living room time and time again, desperate to satisfy that ever-gaping mouth, the diamond-hard beak and the moist, pink, strangely human flesh inside. I need to find a cheaper way to feed Bird. Each time I sprinkle these chia seeds on her strip of a tongue, I think of a pipe whizzing my pound coins away. But they're doing something: she's growing stronger. No longer limping but hopping. Mum once told me toddlers are the most exhausting.

I try to work out what kind of bird she is, scroll endlessly through little square images on my phone. But none of the descriptions seem quite right. I suppose they wouldn't. I'd fall short on a key descriptor anyway: born of woman. I think of Macduff – though he was the opposite. Untimely ripped. The blood and gore of that first laying still lingers too close to the forefront of my mind.

I'm in the bathroom again. Bent double, crying out in pain. There's a strange sound in the background, like a metronome that won't stop, rhythmic and insistent. I push and push and push and this time it's not an egg that comes out, but a giant alarm clock, like the ones in the cartoons, the kind no one's had for years. It's dripping in blood, and each second its ticking is getting louder. I panic, start running it under the tap, while still it gets louder and louder and my contractions get stronger. I decide to get rid of it – I'll take it downstairs, smash it with the casserole, like I thought of doing with the egg but didn't manage. The ticking grows more insistent. But before I even get to the stairs the clock gets immeasurably heavy. The tick-tock-tick-tock is ringing in my ears, it's louder than roadworks, and I see suddenly, with horror, that the minute hand is about to align with the little red dial which tells you when the alarm is set. I can't imagine how loud that will be – tick-tock-tick-tock – and I struggle with the clock, trying to drag it from the landing since it won't be lifted.

Two seconds to go. Tick. Tock. I brace myself for the sound of the alarm.

The ringing is so shrill my eardrums feel like they're about to burst.

And then the clock explodes in my hands. Clots of blood fly everywhere as I'm thrust backwards, down the stairs. For a split second I wonder if Bird is OK.

And then I wake up, my phone alarm ringing, pain tearing at my insides.

⸙

I decide to stop by Mum's, meaning I'll have to leave Bird alone for the first time.

I talk to Bird from the hall as I button up my coat, tell her not to worry, that I'll be back soon. She appears at my feet, cocking her head to one side as if asking a question. I return her to the living room, place her in her towels, trying to make her comfortable. I wonder if she has a clue what I'm saying, stroke her fuzzy plumage so that her eyes close in pleasure. Check again that she has water, that her newspaper toilet is clean. That the window is firmly shut, even though I know she's not capable of escaping yet, even though part of me wishes she were.

When I arrive, Mum's watching a competitive cooking show. The head chef is an impossibly beautiful woman in entirely impractical clothes, with the kind of manicure that no caterer would ever be allowed to cook with, lest the diners end up choking on a talon in the paté. I don't know why she likes this show so much. She's not even a keen cook.

She must have a bit more energy today because she turns off the TV the moment I arrive, leaning to grab her newspaper from the corner table and put it back on her lap as if she's been reading it all along.

Nonetheless, the room is squalid: a graveyard of unwashed mugs on the coffee table, half-opened packets of medicine intermingled with barely read magazines. To my dismay her flowers have wilted even further, starved of the ministrations of their once-zealous human mother.

The doctor's right. Soon I'll have to be here more, perhaps stay here full time. Something to discuss with David when he gets back. I'll add it to my growing list.

I step over a box of what appears to be old (still floury) cookie cutters and give her a hug, trying not to notice how little of her is left in my arms.

She glances at the flowers. I notice the wistful, down-turned look to her eyes and mouth, and without saying anything I go into the kitchen to fill a jug of water. There's a panettone on the side, with a note from Cathy. Good to know she visited. From the sink, I call questions to Mum about her health. She doesn't answer.

I'm suddenly alert. I call again. No reply. Something's happened. Why isn't she responding? I leave the jug on the counter, hurry back, heart racing. But when I get there, she's sitting upright and smiling, the TV on again, and I'll never know whether she didn't hear me or chose not to.

Once I've watered the plants, she beckons to me to sit down next to her and turns the TV off. 'Let's talk about you,' she says. But all I have to say is about Bird. Or my mysterious pains, but I don't want to worry her. 'I haven't asked you for a while – do you think you'd like to have children one day?'

I know she's asking because I brought it up last time. She's trying to be supportive. She means nothing by it. She honestly wants to hear how I feel. She'd support my choice either way. She's that kind of mother, and it's not just the piano lessons. When I said I wanted to study philosophy, she promised me I'd succeed in whatever I put my mind to, even if philosophers weren't very employable. When I then said I was going to train as a project manager, she quickly learnt exactly what that was and read up on 'How to Get Ahead', no matter how many times I told her it was just a route into the music industry. When I told her I'd sold my song, she went out and bought it, not just on CD, but on cassette and vinyl too.

But right now, all I can think about is Bird. I wonder whether to tell Mum everything; she'll be here for me, won't she? Then I remember: now is my time to be here for her.

On the wall the second hand of the clock marches relentlessly on.

I spend all my evenings with Bird because I don't feel I can leave her.

I get a message from Meg: a blurry photo of her on the dance floor, tongue poking wildly from the corner of her mouth.

@the Carpenter's Arms. Join??? xxx

I feed Bird a chia seed, and then I feed her another. I don't notice her getting bigger each day, but somehow by the end of the week she's grown. She's getting stronger, too, and her feathers are smoothing out, cotton wool to smooth satin. She can hop further, stride more confidently, even whistle a few notes.

It's amazing how slowly humans develop by comparison.

'Lia? Lia?' my friend Jess is saying, with a note of impatience. We're at the pub on Sunday afternoon, after the Sunday roast crowd have gone home. It's somewhere between gastro- and old-man pub: retro prints on the walls, but a slot machine in the corner. The heavy wooden table is spread with the contents of a ring binder brought by Jess. She's leaning over it eagerly, spindly fingers spread wide. With her long face, angular nose, grey turtleneck and jerky manner, she looks something like an overexcited heron.

'What? Sorry.'

'Does that sound all right? Can you do that?'

I apologise again. I ask her to repeat. She's been telling me about the plans for her wedding in just over a month's time. Jess has organised every group trip we've ever been on, and most of our weekend plans too. Her fridge has a tidy shopping list always pinned to the front of it, and she'll often pull out her phone mid-conversation to add something to her to-dos. Whereas for me that level of planning would be a busman's holiday.

I'm one of her bridesmaids. She needs me to be 'On Point', she's told me several times. She's promised me no chiffon. But she does need me to pay attention. And I feel bad. I really do. I love Jess. She's been there for me through the break-ups, the failed job interviews, the nightmare bosses. She threw the surprise party when I sold 'Beyond You'. I want her to think I've put in an effort. I want to show her how much I care.

'It sounds lovely,' I tell her. And it does. For her. Not too over the top, nicely personalised. A register office, but one in a nice old building with columns out the front. Bridesmaids in matching colours, but not matching dresses. Dinner, dancing, but no canapés and no endless photos. I know she'll be over the moon, and I'll be over the moon for her.

The problem is I haven't really been listening. Not properly. When she first started speaking, I was thinking about Mum. Hoping the doctor's wrong.

And then Jess said the expression 'like clockwork' and she said it so rhythmically it set a metronome ticking in my head. And now all I can think about is time, how it only goes in one direction, how each day that passes sends us further down the path we're on. I've been thinking about my grandmother, how she—

'Lia?'

Back in the room. A man in the corner woops as coins tumble from the one-armed bandit.

'Lia, would you do a reading at the wedding?' Jess is asking. 'We've chosen something beautiful.'

I almost offer to write her a song. I'd love to find the perfect harmony, lines which would somehow prove my love. But fear sticks the words in my throat. The fear that I'll sit down at my keyboard and nothing will come.

'Of course I'll do a reading. Whatever you want – anything for you,' I say.

'Oh Lia, that'd be *amazing*,' she beams, a happy heron, and her smile warms my heart.

I'm sitting on the living room floor with Bird – a funny way to spend Valentine's. I can't even call David, because he's somewhere mid-air over the Indian Ocean. Not that we've ever gone in for Valentine's. Not really.

I'm rolling a bouncy ball over to Bird, collecting it, and then rolling it again; a game we've played a thousand times over but she never tires of, her black beak scrabbling to bat at it each time it comes her way. The rhythm of the game is so hypnotic my head is almost drooping into sleep, when the doorbell jars me awake. I hurry out of the room, closing the door to make sure Bird stays inside. It's my neighbour Mary, her curly hair a halo of fuzz, holding a package. Must be the birdseed I ordered, but thankfully she doesn't know that. Surreal, really, to see her there holding that package, accomplice to an aberration she knows nothing about.

I accept the package and ask how she's doing. Ordinarily I'd invite her in for tea, and she knows it – I can sense she's lingering, unwilling to turn back from the stoop quite yet.

'I haven't seen you around so much the past few weeks,' she says. 'Keeping well?'

It pains me that I can't let her in. I know how lonely she gets, but besides that she tells good stories, and I can feel the tug of them now. She's also a good listener: calm, non-judgemental, takes your petty worries seriously. I can almost picture myself telling her about Bird; she nods, slowly, letting me tell the whole sorry tale without interruption. *Well, I'm sure it's not as unusual as you think*, she says. *It'll all work out in the end, you'll see.*

But telling her would make Bird real.

The unreal bird caws, clearly unhappy about my absence. I feel bad for shutting her in. Mary tries to peer behind me down the hall.

'What was that?' she asks. My brain scrambles for something plausible. Squeaky door? TV show left on? Babysitting a small child?

In the end I opt for denial.

'I don't know what you mean.'

'I'm sure I heard something.'

'How strange.'

We stand in silence for a moment, cowboys at high noon. I can see her calculating the limits of social nicety.

'I'd love to chat,' I say, and again I feel the tug of close conversation, a confidence shared. I feel awful turning her away, can see the disappointment in her fallen eyes. 'But I'm just in the middle of something, I'm afraid. I'll pop round later.'

Bird caws again and all I can do is say, 'Oh, that is an odd noise; I wonder where it's coming from…' as I close the door on Mary and retreat into the living room, where my avian charge awaits, feathery head raised, beetle eyes glinting as if to say, *Come on Mum, won't you roll that ball one more time?*

'Do you have any regrets?' I ask Mum, and instantly regret it. I can see Doctor Abioye in my mind's eye, or the face of a kindly woman from an imagined care home. *Try to make her dwell on the positives*, they say. *The more someone dwells on their mistakes, the more they wish they had time left to correct them.*

'I wish it wasn't too late for me to ride in a gondola.' I'm winded, thinking of my piano lessons. But she's not even looking at me. She doesn't know that I know. She didn't mean for me to take it this way. 'But you can't turn back time.'

'Do you regret having me?'

As soon as I've said it the words feel too staccato for the room, and I wish I could take them back.

Her face softens, but there's a hint of concern in her eyes.

'Of course not. How could I regret something like that? How could I regret you?' And she hugs me tight.

When we draw apart she frowns, seems to decide it's her turn.

'I do wonder sometimes… Do you ever wish you knew more about your father?'

I wonder how long this has gnawed at her. I know the answer I've always given teachers, friends, hairdressers, but Mum deserves only the greatest sincerity. So I dig deep inside myself to interrogate what's there, what might reveal itself this time. Still I come up with the same response. 'I know he's Sicilian. I know he was a sailor. That's enough for me.' I take her hands, squeeze them in mine. 'It's hard to miss something you never knew. It's you I want to know about, Mum.' And then a notion takes shape which has never found form before. 'Perhaps not knowing him is why I'm so interested to know about Nonna.'

Her eyebrows raise just a fraction.

🥚

I have to travel for a training course. I've been worrying about it, debating whether to pull a sickie, but I've decided I should go. I call Mum, tell her I'll be away for a couple of days. Suggest she lets Maggie and Cathy know, in case she needs help. Engrave a wish in my mind that she'll be OK while I'm gone.

In the living room, I look down at Bird, growing stronger by the day. She's constantly turning her head now, searching the room for – what? Food? Answers? Her wings are beginning to look more like wings, and less like little feathered skink arms that couldn't get an eggshell off the ground. She scurries behind me whenever I'm downstairs, her pitter-patter a whispering percussion. I'd like to leave her behind, go to my training and think of nothing but pie charts and bottom lines, drown in a stupor of data.

But I know without even needing to talk myself through the arguments that I'll be taking Bird with me. The act of feeding her – of keeping her – has wrapped a heavy elastic band around both of us that will only stretch so far.

I kneel down beside her, stroke her velveteen feathers. Her eyes close, reassured by my presence. 'I wouldn't do that to you,' I whisper. Her eyes open, an inquiring look in them. Even I'm not completely sure what I mean.

As I gather the items we'll need for the journey – a towel-lined cardboard box for Bird, her nuts and seeds, heading upstairs to pack my own clothes almost as an afterthought – I feel a dull ache building across my middle that suddenly culminates in a feeling like someone has tugged hard on all my organs at once. I cry out just outside my bedroom door and fall to my knees, then curl up in a ball, my bundled items scattering across the carpet.

I've been lying there for a few minutes, gritting my teeth, when, through my pain-induced haze, I see Bird at eye level. That's the first time she has made it up the stairs. She looks me in the eye, cocks her head to one side – as if to ask why on earth I'm making these moaning sounds – and then tiptoes over to me, pink feet splayed, still watching me closely.

My core is shrinking in on itself, vacuum-packing my stomach muscles so that all I can do is scrunch tighter into my foetal position. Bird rests her tiny head against mine. She's soft and warm. She chirps, a living piccolo. It doesn't make the pain go away, but it reminds me that it *will* go away, just as it has each time before.

I lie there, listening to Bird and praying that sleep will come and relieve me of this pain.

Wondering what's wrong. Wondering what's to blame.

At the training course my pains are gone, but the threat of them lingers, like a gremlin hiding around the corner out of sight, waiting to sink its claws into me. We're in a large room, with corniced ceilings, pub-style carpets and those strange gold-coloured chairs made for stacking, not comfort. A woman with dirty-blond hair is telling me that the pastries were better last year, and I find myself thinking that her boxy mulberry suit makes her look like Hilary Clinton. I want to tell her that I'm not just a project manager, or not a project manager like the rest of them – I work at a music production company, doesn't she know? I want her to look impressed, ask me to tell her something cool about my job. But I don't know how I'd answer that, and someone next to me is talking about their role in delivering the Shard, so I comment on the fruit spread instead.

I wonder how human evolution has come to this: a roomful of people in strange patches of cloth deemed to look 'professional', breathing stale air and deprived of natural light.

I think about how a part of all of us has existed long before us, before our mothers and grandmothers were even born. How, invisible to the naked eye, invisible even to a microscope, in the powerhouses of our cells, we all carry a precious cargo of DNA that has been passed down from generation to generation, century to century, millennium to millennium – DNA that ultimately came from the first woman, back in the garden of Eden, when she first bit into that apple and condemned her daughters to their necessary pain. DNA that made Eve immortal. DNA that each woman can now pass on to her daughter, to pass on to her own daughter after her – should she so choose.

And this is where we've ended up: in a conference centre off the M3.

Word begins to travel from group to group that it's time to return to the lecture theatre, bringing me back into the moment like a thunderclap on a hazy summer's day. I sigh. More PowerPoints and self-serving questions that are really statements, from participants trying to look clever. I pause while everyone around me starts to shuffle towards the double doors. In my head I'm hanging on tiptoe, as if deciding whether to let myself fall, though of course in reality I'm as half-upright as everyone else, maybe a little slump in my shoulders.

I could go up to Bird; I probably should, and in fact I can feel that elastic band tugging at my chest. But something about the image of Bird's sinewy limbs, ever-growing wings, eyes following me round the room with expectation, keeps my feet planted firmly on the pub-pattern carpet. The hotel room seems tiny in my mind – not enough space for the two of us, nowhere to look, nowhere to hide.

Still, the woman hissing at me from the doors that it's time to come back into the training room makes the cinnamon bun I've just eaten return to the back of my throat.

'Not feeling well,' I hiss back. I turn around, clutching my tummy out of habit – but it seems to do the trick. Over my shoulder I see her give a sympathetic smile before turning into the room and closing the doors.

I pad my way through the hotel to the lifts, and up to my room. Bird is there, still in her box, beady eyes and fixed expression, making me cringe. Reluctantly I lift her out of the box and put her on the bed, lying down so I can get a better look. The fact that she's here feels wrong, and even now I ask myself if my eyes are working properly, searching within my own head for the source of this hallucination. But even as I shrink away, try to tell myself she's not really there, I can't take my eyes off her.

She chirrups, seemingly happy to see me, and then clambers over to me, rubbing her head a few times against my arm before curling up and settling down. I stroke her downy head, notice how her increasingly sturdy feathers are turning indigo at the tips. Slowly, her warmth suffuses me, makes me feel that the training downstairs doesn't matter, that project management doesn't matter, that there's only us and this room.

I think that perhaps it is nice to be needed after all.

In Outpatients I get seen by a brunette woman. Wide child-bearing hips (as they call them) and a full bosom. She folds her hands in her lap and looks at me quizzically from her chair while I fuss over my coat and scarf.

'Been feeling any better?' she asks, head tilted to the side like a chicken, hazel eyes wide and staring.

The twinges haven't gone away, but it's possible I've felt them a bit less. Or perhaps dwelt on them a bit less, because of being distracted by Bird.

'Not really,' I say slowly.

'Noticed anything else out of the ordinary?' she asks. I press my lips together, try not to laugh. Her dark brows furrow: she senses something's going on, but can't put her finger on what. Well, that's no surprise.

I look around the office, at the miscellaneous stationery scattered across her desk, the peeling medical posters on the walls, the dusty air vent near the top of the window where a small fan whirs in the wind.

She makes a small throat-clearing noise, and then taps her fingers on the table in alarming mimicry of a beak cracking open an egg. Startled, I flick my gaze back to her.

'You know you can be honest with me, Lia?' she says, smiling kindly. Suddenly I feel bad about appearing dismissive. I notice that her eyes crinkle at the sides, like my mum's. I can picture her with three children crowding around her, clutching at her trouser legs. I wonder if anyone would ever say the same of me.

'I just want to know what's wrong with me.'

She makes one of those facial shrugs, bottom lip brought high, so her chin appears longer than usual, mouth downturned.

I get home, lasagne on my mind. Bird seems ecstatic to see me, hopping around my ankles and flapping her wings in what seems an attempt at flight. I'm ecstatic that another living thing could miss me so much.

I rifle through the Jamie Oliver I barely use until I find the dog-eared insert: a scrap of lined paper I've had since the day I left home, my mum's pencil writing splattered with tomato sauce. Bird patters around me in circles, looking up at me dolefully from the linoleum, reproachful that she's not involved.

I kneel and extract the baking tray from the Jenga tower of pots and pans beneath the oven. Bird flinches at the clattering; I pick up her warm body, funnel my lips and approximate cooing in the hope of soothing her. Then I lay kitchen towel on the counter and place her on it, so she can watch me cook from rib height and I don't have to worry about treading on her.

I take out the tinned tomatoes, more carefully so as not to scare her; the dried pasta sheets, the sausage meat, the watery pot of mozzarella. I drizzle olive oil in the pan, the fan oven gearing itself up noisily in the background.

As I cook, I sing: 'Just you and me, just me and you…'

Bird's poppy-seed eyes follow me as I gently stir the ricotta mixture, channelling my mum as I resist the urge to turn up the heat and get it done more quickly. Steam rises to the ceiling as if from a cauldron. The sausage spits and sizzles, almost ready to mingle in the scarlet marinara.

I layer the lasagne with love, adding the tomato sauce, ricotta and mozzarella in equal measure, deliberate and exact. I add boiled eggs – the Sicilian touch. Then carry it with mittened hands to the oven, check the recipe again for the gestation time, set my timer for forty-five minutes. I reach out my un-mitted hand to Bird, and she gives the fleshy base of my palm an affectionate nibble.

Forty-five minutes later and the kitchen smells of home. My stomach is growling and my heart is hungry. I mitten up again, open the oven door, reach into the hot forge, extract my masterpiece, place it on the counter. I glance at Bird; her poppy-seeds have grown large and reproachful again. She knows she's not the centre of attention.

I take a metal spatula and slice into the stack of aroma before me. It's like a savoury cake on the plate, towering layers and a hint of celebration. I leave the plate behind me on the counter and turn in the galley kitchen to find a fork.

When I turn back, there's an earthy, rancid smell in the air and someone's sick idea of frosting glistening grey and yellow atop my melted parmesan. I look at Bird, but her expression is a picture of innocence; I can almost see the cartoon halo appearing around her head, almost hear its ping.

And then I yank open the cupboard under the sink and retch into the bin.

※

I'm at work when I get the email. I'm supposed to be starting a video call with the IT provider in three minutes: I've made my notes, re-checked the RAG ratings and the risk register, and fixed my hair in the mirror.

I've been trying to avoid coming into the office so I can stay home with Bird, but yesterday Bird was so distracting with her cawing and crying I decided I was better off here, even if my mind does keep wandering back to what she's doing at home; wondering whether she's managed to find the food I left out for her, managed not to fall down the stairs and break her neck, or anything in the house.

Then the email comes, a buzz on my personal phone. I've just got a minute until the call and nothing of use I can do, so I pick it up and open the notification, expecting more wedmin from Jess. Words blur before my eyes. INTERESTED – UNIQUE – SEND ME MORE. My heart starts up a beat. A music publisher I sent a piece to a few months ago liked my demo. A love song, because that's what sells, but not quite.

I'd given up hope of hearing back. Cymbals chime. He wants to float it with some labels, has three in mind. The snare drums join in. He wants to hear more, has given some indications of what he likes, what to lean into, what to bring out. I cross my fingers, remind myself it might not work out. Jump up from my seat, making my colleague opposite look up in alarm. Run into the corridor. A French horn sounds.

No one at work knows about my songwriting. My pitch emails are sent under a pseudonym, just in case. It would be too tragic: Spreadsheet Lia thinking she's Max Martin, not that anyone's heard of him either, even though he's one of the most successful songwriters of our time. Like project managers, songwriters often stay behind the scenes, though the performers would be lost without them.

I savour a moment of joy, trumpets blaring in the orchestra pit of my mind, face and fists scrunched in glee.

And then I return to my desk, place my headset over my ears, and click on to the call, only a few minutes late.

I just hope I can find the time to work on my song in between feeding Bird.

I just hope I can find the thoughts.

When I get home that evening all I want to do is sit at my keyboard and bring new music into being, find ways to rearrange, recalibrate, rewrite the fragments I already have until I discover the song hidden within the song, the song I think I know is there.

But first I have to give Bird attention, because she's been alone all day and she caws for me the moment I walk through the door. I tell myself that while I make her chia mix, I'll play around at the melody and while I spoon feed her I'll give some lyrics a spin, but in the end both tasks are so absorbing, Bird's presence so insistent, I do neither, and all I'm aware of is her gaping beak and the tempo of her gobbling.

Once she's eaten, I leave her with a treat puzzle which claims to provide intellectual stimulation, and head upstairs to my music room. I position myself on my stool, righting my posture and taking mindful breaths as I prepare myself to start – flex my fingers, stretch out my arms. I'll play from memory today, the tune of a Sicilian folk song Mum once played for me from an old record. I switch on the keyboard and position my hands above the keys, body and soul suspended in anticipation of that first note sounding through the air. But before my fingers even meet the keys I hear Bird cawing for me.

I decide to play anyway, leaning into the keys, trying to let the song take me over. For brief moments it does, and I catch the scent of citrus and sea salt on my inward breath. But then the daydream is interrupted by Bird, calling in a different key signature from downstairs like an unwelcome backing track, and the soul-keyboard connection I long for doesn't come. I take up pen and paper, get out my phone to jot down the publisher's feedback in a mind map, hoping that the visualisation of ideas will unlock something. But creativity won't play along. No matter what I do it still feels mechanical, and I know why. My heart can't engage, because it's downstairs with the needy creature crying like an out-of-tune wind instrument.

In the living room, Bird is ignoring the treat puzzle, which lies empty under the armchair.

'I know you know how to come upstairs,' I say to her, offering my hand so she can nibble at the fleshy skin at the base of my palm. Her beak is no longer a dagger to me and despite my annoyance I can't help smiling at this display of affection.

From on top of the bookshelf I take the towel-lined shoebox I've improvised. 'All right, I'll carry you up if that's what you want,' I say. I put both hands around Bird's black downy belly and place her carefully in the box. And then I take her upstairs and place her on the little desk next to my keyboard.

I place a finger on middle C and the note rings out, expectant and clear. Bird remains silent, her head poking out of the box, cocked in curiosity.

And I begin to play.

Bird behaves herself; she sits still, she doesn't make a sound.

But as I play, I find my gaze keeps returning to her.

Wondering again how she got here, why this has happened to me.

Her presence isn't compatible with the day I've had, with its building passes and email niceties and HR processes to follow.

And now here I am carrying on as usual, trying to make all my dreams come true, watched by a bird I hatched myself.

I stop playing. I reach out a hand to touch her silky feathers. She looks at me with what I can only describe as a forlorn expression. She trills, and for a moment it almost sounds like a song.

'You'd rather I was playing with you, wouldn't you?' I say.

She preens beneath my touch.

※

The music publisher suggests we speak. I'm a wreck all day before the call, trying to calm my nerves. I sit at my keyboard stool, Simon and Garfunkel looking down at me moodily from the wall.

The line is crackly, but his words are a symphony. 'I love what you sent,' he says, a Welsh lilt adding cadence to his words. 'The lyrics and the melody match up perfectly. I think this could really appeal. Do you have any particular artists in mind?'

I call David on speakerphone straight afterwards, tapping at my switched-off keyboard with nervous energy; he tells me he's walking along the river in Sydney. My only image of Sydney is the opera house, so I picture that, trying to remind myself it's nighttime where he is.

'Is it difficult to walk upside-down?' I joke. We don't like to take ourselves too seriously.

'Been on any good runs lately?' he asks. *Not since Bird arrived* is the answer, but I don't say so.

'That's amazing!' he says when I tell him about the publisher.

'Nothing's happened yet,' I say hurriedly, already anxious, picturing the call where I have to tell him it's come to nothing.

'That's not true. Someone in the industry has told you they like what you've got. That's huge. Even if they don't go with it, someone else will. You just need a bit of luck.'

'My demos always sound better with you. I wish you were here so we could play together, and you could help me with this feedback,' I say.

'Me too, Lia,' he says, though of course we're both pleased he's there, not here, because this is what he wants to do. 'Send me what you've done so far,' he says. 'I'd love to hear it.'

'I will. And be honest,' I say.

'How honest?' He laughs.

'I want this so much… I hope it goes well tonight,' I say.

'So do I,' he replies, from the Sydney riverside.

Intermingled with my excitement about the publisher come more melancholy strains: Bird and Mum and my pain. David always seems so solid. I want to ask him whether anything ever makes him sad.

And I wish I was there with him, on the other side of the planet, walking upside-down.

⁂

I'm making a chia and sunflower seed mixture for Bird, whistling Disney's 'Zip-a-Dee-Doo-Dah' to myself, when I hear a curious sound. It's almost an echo. I pause, and the echo pauses too. I start to whistle again. And again I hear the notes, but there's something not quite right.

I leave the seeds on the kitchen counter and make my way to the living room, a peculiar sense of dread building from I don't know where. I whistle again.

Zip-a-dee-doo-dah.

Bird is in the middle of the living room carpet, sitting upright, now the size of a wood pigeon, jet feathers iridescent. Her eyes are closed and she's swaying gently from side to side. There's something odd about her stance, as if she's held up by some supernatural force. Since she insinuated herself into my house I've heard her make a cacophony of sounds: chirps, trills, caws and plaintive cries. She's never successfully arranged those into a tune. Until now.

My heart races, double-time. In the kitchen, the air passing through my lips sounded jaunty and confident. From her beak, the notes are discordant, funereal. Suddenly the air is clammy and cold, crypt-like, as if we're deep underground. Shadows undulate in the corners of the room, near the ceiling. Bird keeps going, continuing the tune beyond the fragment I'd been whistling, though much as I rack my brains I can't ever remember whistling it to her before. The shadows grow, seeping like black oil.

With her eyes still closed and her swaying body it's as if she's channelling some other being, from beyond the grave or else unborn, and I want to go over to her and clamp a hand over her beak and make her stop, but I'm rooted to the spot.

Zip-a-dee-doo-dah, she whistles slowly, languidly, and then she stops swaying and her head, which had been turned into the centre of the room, turns towards me, and her eyes are still closed and she's still whistling. Slowly, she takes a step in my direction, eyes still closed, and my blood runs cold.

Without knowing why, I back out, then slam the door shut, trying somehow to keep the shadows inside.

I'm bombarded with fertility adverts. Presumably it's because of my age. The social-media algorithm knows that any woman over thirty yearns in the depths of her soul for biological children and wants to explore every possible way to have them. Clickbait urges me not to leave it too late.

And then there are the photos.

Celebrities with seven sprogs, not a grey hair in sight (they never show the bank-breaking nannies, the entourage).

Friends I know well. Colleagues. Girls I knew years ago but haven't heard from since. Kissing downy heads. Laughing, the wind in their hair. Smiling chubby cheeks.

Maybe I linger on these photos a little too long. Maybe I even seek them out, at 3 a.m. when only the microwave lights are flashing, trying to decode their meaning as if reading ancient hieroglyphs by torchlight.

The thing is, they never show the nappy changes, the late nights, the endless feeds, the crying that won't stop, the early departure from the party, the interrupted cups of coffee, the pick-ups and the drop-offs. The lost music of silence.

They never show the pressure of always Wanting the Best for Them. Of the assumption that Their Needs Come First. You can't take a picture of that.

'When you're a mother,' my colleague is saying, the one who brought her baby in. 'When you're a mother, nothing else matters.'

She looks like she hasn't slept properly in months. I think about how Bird has changed my life, how much easier she is than a baby. I wonder not for the first or even tenth time how they do it – these parents who only skirt around their REM cycles, show up to a full day's work, then find it within themselves to lavish love on their little one.

We're washing our mugs at the tea point towards the end of the day, purple 'Pentatonic' shouting at us from the wall opposite. I'd asked what it was like to be back at work, genuinely baffled by the mechanics of the operation. As a project manager, I know there aren't enough hours in the day. The Gantt chart doesn't add up.

'What do you mean?'

'You get a new perspective on things. I can't explain it.'

I wonder if that's what I need. Perspective. Maybe if I could work out what mattered, Bird would go away.

'Life isn't just about work any more. You have to think about something bigger than yourself, you have to stop being selfish,' this colleague is saying. My sympathy starts to ebb away. 'It's a twenty-four-hour responsibility,' she continues, eyes wide as if trying to impress this simple fact on me, as if it wasn't obvious. 'It's not easy when you're a mum. Your children must come first. You have to make sacrifices.'

I wonder if I should genuflect.

Suddenly she grabs my hand. Hers is clammy, like a child's – except how would I know?

'Have you decided yet?' she asks me earnestly, chewing her thumbnail. She's clearly worried I'll make the 'wrong' decision.

I'm tempted to tell her about my pain. I wonder how she'd feel if someone responded that they *couldn't*, imagine using the word 'barren', feel it rolling off my tongue, see her eyes widen and then dim with pity. Pity I don't know if I deserve.

'You do seem different,' I say, and even as I say it I'm not sure whether I mean it as a compliment, although I hope she'll take it that way.

I excuse myself and return to my desk, shut down Excel as I normally would and head home, not to compose as I normally would, but to look after Bird – because, in the words of my colleague, life isn't just about work any more.

As I walk home from the station, trying to avoid the cracks in the pavement, I see children everywhere. I've been seeing birds everywhere too, ever since Bird's hatching.

There's a little girl standing by a park bench, trying to tie her laces. Her hair floats in the fading evening sun, hazy like the wings of a hummingbird. She looks a bit like Jess. 'Grandma, come see,' she says in a voice unworn by years. I smile. A daughter like her I could almost imagine…

Then a boy, a little older – perhaps seven – flailing as his dad tries to get him into a car. His face is an angry red, his screaming grating. The other side of the coin.

I think about how that's exactly what parenthood is: a toss-up, a leap into the unknown. We congratulate the pregnant couple, think of the best-case scenario, but in reality the whole process is fraught with risk.

Safa once asked if it worried me, not knowing the specifics of 50% of my basic ingredients: whether I have 'good genes', whatever that means. I know my father was Sicilian, but she's right, I don't know what my odds are in this game. Then again, does anyone? There will always be mysterious pains that strike us down. Broken families spread across continents. Offspring who won't carry on the family name.

David said one child could fit into our life, but that's presuming no 'complications'. The risks of which continue all the way into adulthood, as far as I can see, because you never know what's going to happen, how they'll turn out, what kind of support they'll need. As if becoming a mother wasn't complicated enough as it is.

The boy and his father drive off, their faces twisted into frowns. The girl and her grandmother have gone to queue for ice-cream, though it's not the season.

Most of all I think about how, if it wasn't for Bird, I wouldn't need to be anywhere right now. I could stop here, on this paving stone, and stand and watch how the sun falls just so between the buildings, or turn around, go to the park, drop it all and take a train to the seaside. How my time is my own. Or was, until my head was stuffed with feathers. I hear cawing and so I keep walking, back home, back towards Bird. I have the sense that I'd be able to hear her even in Whitstable, even over the rushing of the tide.

Have you decided yet? My colleague's words echo around my mind like water dripping in a well, unstoppable and ever constant. Why the 'yet' – what is she implying – don't I still have time?

I think of Mum. I think of her years. I think of children without grandparents, grandparents without grandchildren. I think of how eggs are first formed in the ovaries of the foetus, so that some iteration of me, no wider than a hair, has existed ever since my mother came into being in the womb of my grandmother.

I turn the corner on to my street. Discarded paper and fast-food cartons litter the pavement at intervals. I picture myself in old age, see myself like Mum, struggling to make a cup of tea and no one there to make it for me. Or maybe there is someone in the picture. David. Meg. A carer. I think of another friend, who moved to Australia. The time she rang me up in the middle of the night because her dad had fallen, and she was ten thousand miles of heartache away. I rushed to the hospital, of course I did – nothing to stop me, not David nor a small child nor a job I'm particularly passionate about nor thirty-six hours of travelling in my way. I held his hand while they wheeled him into the operating theatre. I held the phone to his ear so she could talk to him while he took his last breaths.

I reach our house. It's an OK house, not big, but plenty of space for one person or two. Any more, and it might start to feel crowded. Any more, and I'd have to get rid of my music room. My sanctuary, where I should be spending all my time working on my song. I've got past the opening bars, am now searching for the chorus, trying to see how many facets can be captured by the word *love*.

I turn the key in the lock and enter. A stray feather is lying on the mat, black silk against the coarse brown. A faint sound wafts down the stairs from the music room and I traipse up the stairs, as if summoned.

As I approach the landing I discern middle C resonating from the keyboard. A cold coagulation runs from my skull down my spine. The music room door is slightly ajar, but I almost don't dare open it further. My hand seems to have more courage because it reaches out in front of me, flat on the white wood, pushing inwards.

Bird is sitting on the panel of the keyboard. When she sees me she leans forward all the way, a diver plunging into the lagoon, so that her beak touches the C and her weight presses it down. It rings out again. She returns to her upright position.

I suppose middle C is the note she's seen me play the most, pressing it at the start of each session and then again when I lose my train of thought and again when I want to start over. It's an anchor. The fact that she both managed to find it, and worked out how to turn the keyboard on, is astounding.

She dives again, and again the C hangs expectantly in the air. Though I know she doesn't have eyebrows, it's almost as if hers are raised – as if she's saying, *Well, come on then, show us what you've got.*

This time I'm not scared. I'm proud.

I sit down at the keyboard, and middle C is waiting.

I should be songwriting, but Bird seems weighed down with melancholy and it sits heavy on my heart. I set myself up cross-legged in the living room again, watching her. She lacks her usual energy, her head moving only barely, as if through tar. There's something languid in her limbs too.

'What's wrong, my little one?' I ask, moving to lie on my front, arms folded beneath my chin, so I can meet her at eye level. She blinks – not by closing her eyes, like humans do, but with her milky third eyelid that slides horizontally from one corner of her eye to the other like a windscreen cover, pupils still fixed on my own. I've seen her do this plenty of times now, but nonetheless I can't help but shiver. It's so reptilian; it makes me think of a basking adder, tongue flicking in and out as it tastes its prey on the air.

I wonder if this is why I haven't given Bird a name, though it's over two weeks since she hatched. There's a power in naming, a significance to it that I've afforded the goldfinch in my garden (Bob Dylan), my aloe vera plant (Leonard Cohen) and the spot I had that wouldn't go away for months (Aunt Mabel). And yet Bird remains as she is – a description more than a name, an adjective as much as a generic noun.

'What would you like to be called?' I ask her, and that translucent film appears again, quick as a flash, left-to-right, like some kind of coded message. But as soon as I turn my mind to names, I feel a kind of tightening in my chest and something approaching the gag reflex at the back of my throat, and I go to the power button and press 'shutdown' on the thought.

Time to write.

I cup my hands in front of her so that she can climb into them, claws pricking me cleanly as she grips on, and carry her upstairs. Placing her on the windowsill, I sit on my keyboard stool. I close my eyes for a moment, trying to get in the zone, then open my eyes and see she's closed hers too, this time with no sense of threat. My fingers rap on the control panel, trying to find the rhythm of the chorus, something which keeps time with my heart. From the ledge, she raps her beak on the control panel like a woodpecker, keeping time too. And then I whistle my opening note and she whistles back, but this time it's melodious and bright, and when I sway she sways, and soon we're whistling in tune with each other.

Except I can't take my eyes off Bird, and I can't get past those first three notes. Downstairs she had seemed so Other; here, in the music room, it's easier to believe she hatched from me. I begin to examine her, looking for some kind of resemblance, anything to confirm that she came from me and there's something to bind us together beyond misfortune and wild happenstance. Her sharp beak makes me think of all the times I've said things, then wished them unsaid. Looking at her ropey pink fingers I find myself flexing my own, poised to trill over the piano keys, grasping at something long yearned for but ever intangible and out of reach. But beyond these imaginings there's little evidence of me.

Besides, her feathers are black, and my hair is dishwater blond.

🥚

When I arrive to see Mum the living room is in a different kind of chaos to normal. All the usual artefacts are in their usual places – the books piled haphazardly at all kinds of angles, the spider plants that trail across the floor, the trinkets collected over too many weekends spent browsing Portobello Road covering every inch of every surface. But today there's something else: large leather-bound books left open on the sofa and coffee table, and little rectangles of white paper with dark patches in the middle scattered about. They're black-and-white photographs, much older than the ones dotting the room in frames.

'You want to know about your grandmother,' says Mum. She's buzzing today, her voice lilting, her hands aflight.

'Yes?' I say, raising an eyebrow.

'Come, come,' she says, flapping her hand and kneeling beside the coffee table. I sink into the soft cushions of the sofa.

'I wish I could have taken you there,' she says. 'Maybe you'll go one day.' She hands me an old photo, showing box-like houses lining a narrow street. In one corner an old woman dressed all in black sits on a stoop, looking away from the camera.

Then another photo. Another woman wearing black in front of a church façade standing tall and proud. It looks white, but it's hard to be sure in monochrome.

'Is this her?' I ask.

'Your great-grandmother,' Mum says hastily, as if already desperate to move on from the topic of her mother, even though she's the one who brought her up.

'How big was the village?' I ask.

'Now? Less than eight hundred people. Then? Something over a thousand.'

That's smaller than my secondary school. I swallow, stroke the image of this woman whose genes I carry. What connects us other than that? A bright-coloured blanket? A love of cannoli? Not even a family name.

'Why did she leave?' I ask. I don't mean my great-grandmother, as she wasn't the one who left, I mean her daughter, my grandmother. But it seems best not to reference her directly, to let Mum choose what she wants to share.

'They were very poor,' Mum says. She hands me more photos: dusty children, scrawny cattle, and everywhere women in black. 'After someone died, they wore mourning clothes for at least three years, sometimes the rest of their lives,' Mum explains. 'And someone had always died.'

That night, my dreams are filled with voices, words and sounds I've never heard before: my brain scrabbling at Sicilian. The woman from the picture walks ahead of me, and I keep trying to catch up with her, but for every step I take, she takes another step further away. At last I reach her, tap her on a black-clad shoulder. She turns around, and for a moment I'm terrified, but then she smiles, an uncomplicated smile from a weathered face. A face which contains traces of my mother's, perhaps even of my own.

She takes my hand, and I feel a power pulsing through me, an insistent blue light. 'From me to you,' she says, cupping my hands in hers.

I feel this light she has entrusted me with is something I must protect, cherish and pass on to someone else. Suddenly I see my grandmother, and my mother, all holding the light and passing it on to me.

'Will you carry it for us?' my mother asks.

I know I want to. I turn, to see if there is someone, a little girl, or a little boy, perhaps, David's spitting image, to whom I can pass this light. But there's no one there, and instead I open my mouth and music emerges. It's blue and glowing too, and it suffuses the room, a song full of words and sounds I don't recognise, and it's the most beautiful song I've ever heard.

I wake up the next morning with a capriccio playing in my head and as I go about my morning routine I become aware of a presence. It's not physical, watching me from the edge of the bath like Bird, but rather a hidden force nestling somewhere between my eyes while I brush my teeth. I make my way down the stairs, a little more unsteady on my feet than usual. I make it to the kitchen and start boiling the kettle. As the steam rises, I realise what it is I'm carrying: the spirit of my grandmother. More so than usual, anyway. My skin isn't quite her olive hue, and my tattered dressing gown can't compare to her luxurious white coat. But I suppose a part of her is always with me.

I can feel her today much more than I ever have: her pride, her ambition, her pizzazz. As I pick an apple from the bowl, enjoy its waxy coolness beneath my fingertips. As I allow myself to watch the goldfinch in the garden, hopping from branch to branch, because I can. In these moments of stillness, I can feel her longing tugging at me; these are luxuries she could not afford.

She doesn't like Bird, that's clear. The closer I get to her the more revulsed my nonna feels. So I spend the morning avoiding Bird, giving the living room a wide berth, slipping past so her black shape is never more than at the periphery of my vision.

*

'They still don't know what's wrong with me,' my friend from HR is saying. We're sitting in a 'breakout space', surrounded by the kind of padding you'd normally expect in an asylum.

She's clutching at her abdomen, as if hoping she can summon a baby through the pressure of her palm. Her bobbed hair hangs lifelessly around her face, wan as instant porridge. Over the past few months, she's wilted. She used to be the one cracking jokes in meetings, catching my eye every time the Head of HR said 'pacifically'. But the doctor's appointments, tests, medicine have taken their toll. She's been channelling all her energy to her womb, to hothousing embryos, hoping that one – just one – will stick around. She has an addict's relationship with hope; each time the crash is worse than the last, but each time she goes crawling back.

I wish I could do something for her. I've no way of knowing if I'm fertile, unless you count egg-brooding – my abdominal pains weigh on my mind – but I have a mad urge to offer myself up as a surrogate, if it'll get her what she wants.

I want to tell her that there are other options; there are children out there in need of homes, chicks in need of nests. I also want to tell her: 'Don't worry about it. There are other things in life.' But I can see the longing in her eyes; that's not what she's been told. That's not what she feels deep inside.

I know that now is not the time, not yet, anyway, and I clutch my own hips superstitiously, as if summoning some pagan fertility goddess upon her.

She seems to tire of the subject, or at least wants to forget about beating the clock for a little while. 'What about you and David?' she asks, putting my heart beneath a magnifying glass.

I think of Bird and my increasing desire to be rid of her, my fear of how it will feel to be left behind. I think of my pain, and what it might mean, and how I don't know how that makes me feel. I don't know how to answer her, but if I did, I wouldn't be able to tell her the truth. It would feel too callous, rubbing salt in the wound. In the vicinity of her womb it would feel like casting the evil eye.

I glance around quickly, suddenly conscious we're open-plan and anyone could walk past.

'Oh, you know – not yet,' I say hurriedly, trying to think how to change the subject. Wondering if Bird will turn out to be friend or foe. Wondering what she's doing right now.

But she won't let me. She takes my hand in hers, squeezes it tight. Looks me intensely in the eyes, as if trying to reach through time to her former self.

'Don't leave it too late.'

Perhaps there's something wrong with me, too, I think. Not just with my womb. With my heart.

※

It's two weeks since the publisher asked me to send more, but between Bird, Mum and my own pain, I'm still stuck on the chorus, trying to find a combination of notes and lyrics that doesn't feel derivative, the fragments of gold hiding in the sludge, *love is a red red rose* playing on repeat in my mind.

At times like this I feel worthless. This is the one thing I've always wanted to achieve in life – the thing I want to look back on when I'm lying on my deathbed – and yet I'm not able to find time for it, and though Bird hasn't helped, I can't lay all the blame at her taloned feet. I was no stranger to procrastination even before she arrived.

I've read about the poets and songwriters who get up at four every morning so they can fit creative work around day jobs or children, and hearing about them should inspire me. Instead, I feel worse. Where are my reserves of determination? Perhaps some people aren't meant to have it all.

On Saturday I set my alarm early and resist the urge to snooze. I fill the cafetière all the way to the top and wait until the whole kitchen smells of fresh roast beans, before placing my hand on the plunger and forcing it down. I set myself up in the music room, and place Bird in her box in the doorway, my back turned so she can see me but I can't see her, and with my head clear, not a glance at social media, I compose myself, and I begin to play.

The first notes are tentative steps, tremulous and unassuming. But freed from distraction, they grow in confidence, rounded edges filling the room. Finally, like swallows finding their formation in the summer sky, the chorus takes shape.

It soars.

⊛

Safa's baby has come. A March birthday. We're sitting on her balcony, which overlooks a main road but is pleasant in its own way. I can see London Fields in the distance, scrubby broccoli trees and patchwork grass, greening again in the spring sun. She's cradling baby Yasmin in her arms. Yasmin is perfect. Her eyelashes are silk, her eyelids dun petals. Her cheeks are like a cherub's. Her dusky skin is soft, and her chubby little arms are squishy to touch. I feel a rush of love for this baby, this daughter of Safa's. I want the best for her, I want her to grow up to be whatever she wants to be. I want to protect her. I want to see her laugh, hear her find words, teach her songs and then sing them with her. I want the doctors to tell me I'm going to be fine, so I can sit with Safa when we have wrinkles on our faces and our boobs have dropped, and drink tea and talk about Yasmin's latest adventures.

'If you don't have children, don't you worry you'll regret it?' Safa asks.

I look down at Yasmin, a warm fuzzy feeling inside, like in the movies. And then I think of the last time I was stressed, the last time I was in pain. I remember my bad days, the days I want to curl up and never get out of bed. The days that are for recharging. The days when I don't know who I want to be. The days when my own company is too much.

I think of how hard it is to make music, to find your own tune and bring it to life. How hard it was before Bird; how much harder it's become.

'Sometimes. But I'd rather regret not having children than have them and regret it,' I say. Safa jerks her head back, looking up at me. My words have pulled her up short. I feel guilty; I've said the wrong thing.

But she's the one who asked.

'Laaaaadies and gentlemen, good evening and welcome to This Was Your Life, the show where we tot up the scales and then the audience decides – were you a success or a total flop? And tonight, ladies and gentlemen, we've got… Lia! Now, Lia, what would you say is your life's greatest achievement?'

Bright lights in my eyes, their heat making me sweat. A morass of indistinguishable faces. Me and this leering man in a sequined suit, his voice booming out into the darkness. It ranges high and low like the ringmaster of a circus.

'I… erm…' I stammer.

'Did you become an award-winning songwriter?' He's half speaking to me, half to the audience, his mouth doing gymnastics to talk and smile at the same time.

'Well no, but—'

'Did you found a homeless shelter?'

'No, but the soup kitchen—'

'Did you get to the dizzy heights of your fabulous career?'

'Actually, it was pretty—'

'OK, OK, so you didn't do those things. But you had a child, right? You performed the ultimate miracle – you brought life into this world?' He's close to me now, a hand gripping my shoulder, making my skin crawl. His eyes shine with tears.

'Well, actually—'

'Aaaaaand time's up. Now it's for you, the audience, to decide. Was Lia a success, or was she a total flop? Fingers on buzzers…'

The lights go dark.

I don't know what's happened, but I can see something's not right. As much as I never asked for Bird, never wanted her, I feel panic start to rise in my throat.

She's been hopping more and more confidently around the living room. And she's been getting stronger. But now she's lying on her side; it's clear she fell while I was out. And her leg is twisted strangely. There's an acrid smell in the air, and a dark puddle beside her that I can't bring myself to approach just yet.

To my slight surprise, I'm sick with worry. I try to work out if it's because I care about her, or because I feel responsible. Having started to look after her, I feel I've entered into some kind of contract, though I don't know with whom. If I lose her now, I've failed. Something deep inside me needs to see this through.

I rush over to crouch on the carpet beside her. She's much bigger now, but I can still cup her in my hands. Her eyelids are half closed, as if the world is too much to bear. The smell of her vomit reaches my nostrils. I try not to retch. Close up, I can see her breathing has quickened.

I feel a worrying twinge of pain in my abdomen but try to ignore it. I have something important to do.

I reach out a hand, fingertips then palms making contact with her plush feathers. I place her gingerly in amongst the towels, shushing that it'll be OK, and rush upstairs, rummaging in a cupboard, throwing things out into the hall, not caring where they land. I find a cardboard box and tip the shoes out. This will do. Back downstairs again, check she's still breathing (faintly as dying flames) and I've got her in the box, covering her up so I can take her outside without anyone seeing.

'This is it. Time to meet the outside world.'

I don't need to tell anyone where she came from. I start to chew my lip, so hard that I taste blood. I hope she's a normal, native kind of bird.

I must have walked past the vet thousands of times, my eye drawn to the pets waiting in the window: Shih Tzus and Dobermanns on leads, Persians and plain brown tabbies just visible in their baskets. They look just as uncomfortable as human patients, eyeing each other up, wondering who will be seen first and trying not to get too close for fear of catching something. When I arrive, panting, my shoebox in hand, I spot through the glass that every seat in the waiting room is taken, by human or animal. Perhaps I should have called ahead.

A chime sounds as I enter, the first few notes of 'How Much Is that Doggy in the Window?'.

'It's an emergency,' I say loudly and – I hope – importantly, striding up to the counter where the top of a head is visible. The counter reaches to my chest; the head is a man sitting behind it. Looking down at him, I register the bored expression on his face. He's barely more than a teenager, acne-covered forehead and skinny shoulders his green vet-branded T-shirt hangs off.

'What's the emergency?' he says, arms folded, looking at the box with his eyebrows raised, as if challenging me to pull a magical creature out of it. Little does he know.

'My bird—' I begin breathlessly, but he cuts me off.

'We don't really do birds here,' he says, standing up and leaning his hands on the desk under his side of the counter. He unfolds his arms just enough to wave one hand listlessly in a circle, as if to say, 'Look.' And he's right, of course – I've never seen a single bird here, in amongst the Shih Tzus.

My heart sinks. 'Don't really, or don't?' I ask, hand pressing down on top of the shoebox.

Arms refolded, he sighs and looks up at the ceiling, shoulders sagging. 'What type of bird is it?' he says.

I falter. 'It's...' I fumble, scrambling to open the shoebox. 'It's a wild—'

But before I can finish, he yelps, suddenly woken from his stupor of indifference. My hand slams shut on the box and I pull it to my chest, hoping the sound hasn't scared Bird.

He's taken a full step back from his desk, his back now against the wall.

'Get it out of here!' he jabbers, his voice suddenly an octave higher, his hands waving frantically, shooing me like an animal.

'But—' I plead, desperately.

'Look,' he says, and he leans over the counter towards me, now speaking in a low voice, looking furtively at the other customers. 'Wild animals have all sorts of diseases. We can't risk those in here. There's a bird sanctuary in Sidcup. How bad is it? If needs be, we can put it to sleep.'

'No!' I cry out, surprising myself again, clutching Bird in her box closer to my chest. A couple of waiting customers glare at me. He glares twice as hard.

'Then get out,' he hisses between clenched teeth. I turn and flee, hurrying past the customers, out on to the windy pavement.

Once outside I dare to lift the lid to check on Bird. There's no more vomit, despite all the motion, which I find reassuring, though I don't know if I should. Lid restored, I take out my phone and use one hand to check the journey to Sidcup. It's two buses and over an hour of travel. Except with the reliability of buses at this time of day, I bet it'll be closer to two. This is the last thing I want to be doing with my afternoon. My list of errands – not just for me, but for Mum and Mary and Bird herself – swims before my eyes and then melts away. Sidcup it is.

And then my phone rings. I shiver, wishing I hadn't left my coat at home. It seems what we thought was spring was still winter in disguise. The sound at the other end is muffled but I recognise the voice of my mother's doctor.

'She's had a stroke, Lia,' she says.

One word which sets the world askew, as if tectonic plates are shifting around me, a fault line running right through south-east London.

'She's not doing well. I think you should come.'

I clutch the box tighter, worried I might drop it; I feel weak, the earthquake trembling up from the soles of my feet, through my knees and right to my quivering heart.

'But what happened?'

'These things happen. At her age.'

As if that's the only explanation needed. As if that means it doesn't matter. As if there aren't still countless things I want to do, and tell her about. Things I want her to be proud of. I haven't even told her about Bird. I haven't even decided whether to give her grandchildren.

Bird. She needs me. She needs Sidcup.

I have to go to the hospital — I'll never forgive myself if I don't make it to Mum in time. But A&E isn't the place for Bird, and the receptionist has spooked me with his talk of diseases. I think of Mum, teetering on the edge.

For a mad moment I think of going back inside, asking them to end it all here and now, or leaving Bird on a doorstep for someone else to decide, but the way my heart leapt and my lips said 'no' without even asking me, tells me I can't. I'm bound to Bird now. Somehow, I feel something bad will happen if I leave Bird behind. Bird is of my flesh, after all. Bird is perhaps even of my soul.

I'll take her home. She was looking better already, I tell myself. I'll take her home and leave her, just for an hour or two, wrapped up warm, with plenty of water. Don't they say that hydration is the cure to all ills?

I taste blood on my lip all over again.

I'll go to Mum. But first, I turn my steps uphill, in the opposite direction from the hospital.

I'll take Bird home. I have to find out how this ends.

A darkened room, curtains drawn as if too much light could scare what's left of life away. Mum laid flat in the middle, her shrunken face poking out from neatly tucked sheets. I'd rather she were lost in duvets, soft waves of luxury down instead of these puritan woollen blankets.

When I arrive, Mum stirs and curls into a foetal position. The ambrosia of relief has a vinegary aftertaste: I never wanted to see her like this. She reaches out her hand, seemingly the only way she knows to greet me. When I take it in mine it's as soft as a baby's. I kiss her downy hair and whisper that I'll be there as long as she wants me. And then I squeeze her hand and silently beg her not to go. She wraps her fingers around mine, gesturing to me to come closer. I take a chair and sit beside her at the head of the bed, singing her the Sicilian lullaby she's always sung for me.

Fa la ninna, fa la nanna, nella braccia della mamma.
Go to sleep, go to sleep, in your mother's arms you'll keep.

She smiles at me, but it's as if she's smiling from another time, a time already passed, or perhaps that has never been.

'How are you doing, Mum? Can you hear me?'

'Of course I can hear you!' she says: a flash of her old fire, though her words blur into each other.

'The nurses say you're doing very well,' I say, not sure how to navigate this situation, regurgitating phrases I've heard in films. What would she say if it were me?

'Do they, now?'

She's still curled up, but it's clear she wants me to understand that though her body may be weak, her mind is all there.

'Can I do anything for you? To make you feel better?' I say, trying a different tack.

'Talk to me…' she says, her words slurring into a soup.

Suddenly, selfishly, I want to know what it is she's always refused to tell me about my grandmother. A voice in my head tells me it's not the right time to ask, but another voice tells me there may be no time better.

'Come on then, talk to me!' she says impatiently, her animated tone incongruous with her motionless body.

She doesn't want to be patronised, I tell myself. And so, I ask. 'Mum, where is she? Where's your mother? And why did you leave her?'

Mum's voice is rough as crumbled biscotti, and her response is cryptic. 'My mother didn't do what a mother should.'

The dark hospital room is too warm for me, but I know she needs it, so I tuck the blankets higher around her shoulders.

'But what do you mean? What exactly?'

She looks back at me, seemingly torn. I don't know if it's me she's trying to protect, or her mother.

'Your nonna was an actress,' she says slowly, feeling her way.

'I know that.'

'Her career was very important to her,' Mum says. I get the sense she's both choosing her words carefully, rummaging for scrabble tiles, and then delivering them effortlessly, composing them letter by letter in a mix of English and Italian, conscious of the errors in her delivery, the way what she's saying is blurring at the edges, between her different languages, between her different lives. But as she speaks she seems to find more energy inside herself. She picks up a wind. 'It meant I rarely saw her. Your grandfather had always supported her acting, and unusually for their time, he was the one to brush my hair and tuck me into bed. But after tuberculosis took him, she started leaving me on the coast with her sister-in-law, your great aunt Antonella, who had no children of her own. First for days, then weeks. Then she stopped coming back.'

I gasp. 'She abandoned you?'

'I'd still get presents from her at Christmas, and on my birthday – tennis shoes and silver hoop earrings and once a fur muffler, things none of my school friends could even dream of.' She pauses for breath. I have to concentrate to discern the words, her speech a mixture of wavering sounds and half-swallowed consonants. 'And sometimes, she'd show up for a few hours, buy me ice cream and ask me about my favourite things. But then she'd be gone again, and I'd be left holding my breath each time I came home from school, wondering whether or not she'd be there.'

I try to suppress the thought that Mum has only accepted to tell me all this now because she thinks she won't get another chance.

'When I was grown-up, things changed. Suddenly she had an opinion on everything in my life, when she'd never seemed that interested before. And then I got pregnant.'

She seems to decide that's enough. We sit in silence for a few minutes, only the hum of the machines by her bed providing a hollow backing track.

'How come I've never met Antonella – if she raised you?' I ask, trying to pick up the conversation again, navigate the maze of Mum's feelings about her mother.

'She died a long time ago, *cara*. Otherwise you'd have known her, I can promise you that.'

I briefly think that I should go home, to check on Bird, but I can't resist asking one more question. 'What about your mother – were you in touch with her before she died? Do you know where she was? Did she die alone?'

Here, with my mother lying in her hospital bed, I'm again struck that when my mother dies, so will my grandmother Chiara, finally, and now this woman Antonella too, only newly brought back to life by my mother's words. All that will be known of my grandmother will be that she dreamt of the silver screen, and that she sang '*Fa la ninna nella braccia della mamma*'. And all that will be known of Antonella is this quivering starting note. Until I, too, am gone, and even these faint echoes die away.

My mother twists her mouth to the side.

'I don't know,' she says in Italian, her voice weak and stuttering. 'I didn't stay in touch.' And then, as if to justify herself, or perhaps finding another thread: 'You asked if I have any regrets. I used to say to myself, There must be more to this life. But then I started to come home from the shop and see you every night, and hold your warm little hand in mine, and feel that electricity pulsing up through my arm and right into my heart, see your eyes full of a universe of possibilities, and I would say to myself – *this* is why I'm here.' She pauses, recovering from the exertion of speaking. 'This is what the hard work, the pain, the blood, sweat and tears are for.'

And then it's as if we're both looking at each other from opposite sides of a mirror, and in this warm, dark room we clasp each other's hands, and we're floating, together.

When I get home to find Bird sleeping peacefully in her box, I'm surprised to feel not relieved, but deflated. My limbs feel heavier than usual as I do all the things I have to do for her: replacing the newspaper in her toilet box; replenishing her chia seeds and her water; tidying her nest. I examine the shape of Bird's head, her tail. Her beak seems sturdier, her wingspan longer: is there a hint of albatross in her blood?

I think back to the vet's, try to recapture that rush I felt, the way that single word sounded out so clearly from my throat, across the room. Adrenaline was storming through my veins; here at home, my blood seems thinner, as if there's not enough flowing to muster strong emotion. If anything serious had happened to Bird it would have been a tragedy, a calamity; how could I bear for anything to happen to such a defenceless creature? When I thought she might die, I had this awful feeling that I wasn't ready to say goodbye, or perhaps that I didn't know what I would say in those final moments.

But there was also a small part of me, somewhere hidden where I don't like to admit, that would have felt a little lighter. After all, I've done everything I could. It wouldn't be my fault if something happened to her. Not fault but fate.

I sit in the living room with her. I guess she's going to be fine: nothing more than an upset stomach, it seems. I've no way of knowing if her speech is slurred, though I could listen to hear if she sings differently, I suppose. I do resent her good health a little. Why should she turn out to be fine, when Mum might never recover easy speech, might never walk again? I hate Bird in this moment, and I hate myself for spending even a minute with Bird that I could spend with Mum. I bargain with the Devil, the way I used to do when I was a child, the way my mum told me

I never should: *Let Mum out of hospital and you can have Bird*, I tell Him. *Let Mum out of hospital and you can have me.*

I tell Bird that I'm terrified I'll lose my mother, that I don't want to be alone in the world. That every moment with Mum is borrowed time.

Bird nestles beside me on the sofa, feathers warm but toughening for flight, wings growing wide and strong. But of course she doesn't say a word.

I dream I'm somewhere dark. Strange sounds reverberate through flesh and fluid, an experimental prelude to the symphony of life.

I'm not yet born. I crouch in this beating dark cubby hole of a hideout, sucking my thumb, sometimes kicking, and occasionally laughing. Here I'm safe, or at least as safe as my mother. If anything happens to my mother it will happen to me, in the same way that nothing can happen to me without it happening to my mother.

Most importantly, I have no choices. No decisions to make. There is only one place to be, and that is here. One day I'll be expelled, but that won't be through any exercise of my executive function, rather an age-old process of the body knowing the time is ripe and setting an earthquake in motion.

Neither I nor my mother get to choose when that is.

With no choices, I can have no regrets. I can just be, waiting to see what the world will thrust upon me, going with the flow, in sync with the rhythm of millennia.

A dull ache wakes me in the middle of the night. A familiar darkness.

I clench my fist, use it to create pressure, try to knead the pain away. In the hope of distracting myself, I venture first a toe and then a whole leg out from under my blanket, get out of bed, tiptoe down to where Bird is sleeping peacefully, legs folded beneath her and head nestled in folded wings. I boil the kettle, hoping it won't wake her. Pour the steaming water down the neck of a hot-water bottle. Tiptoe back up to bed. Lie, foetal, clutching the warm packet to me. Drift into half-dreams that never fully embrace.

I once read that mother and baby exchange DNA while the baby is in the womb. Not only does the mother's body pass nourishment through one tube and remove impurities from another, but as this circling continues, so too does the circulation of cells. Tiny specks that were once part of the mother start to spin inside her baby, and tiny specks that were once part of the baby start to spin inside her. Where she needs healing, they heal. If other types of cells are needed, they mutate.

Soon these cells are embedded in her organs, carrying the DNA of her unborn child. A complex code of dancing pairs that don't match those in the rest of the mother's cells. A slightly different tune.

Meanwhile, the mum's DNA is circling inside her unborn child. Not half of it – all of it, in some specific cells whirling their way round her baby's body.

Eventually, when mum and baby separate, nourishment and purification become messier, tawdrier, harder work. And it's true, sometimes, that toil leads to strife, sees daughter push mother away, sees the distance between them grow and grow.

But the dance continues inside each of them, mother's dance in daughter, daughter's dance in mother, whether they want it to or not.

Now I have two women in my head: Chiara, the woman who birthed my mother, and Antonella, the one who accepted her into her nest. They jostle for space with Bird, turning round and round like one of those Christmas candleholders wherever I go. Chiara-Antonella-Bird. Chiara-Antonella-Bird. The carousel tends to get stuck on Bird, because Bird is the one who's actually here, flesh and feathers, piercing me with her unnerving gaze, whose caws are audible wherever I am in the house and sometimes even when I'm far from home.

But then I'll be at the shops and walk past a shelf of citrus fruit and suddenly it'll be Chiara keeping time again. Or see an older woman with a younger child and think of Aunt Antonella, trying to give form to the shapeless image in my mind.

Chiara's presence is like a haunting, the ghost of a woman trying to find her own way in life, who perhaps never wanted a daughter but was never given the choice.

Antonella's spirit is more unassuming, maybe because I have no mental picture of her, nothing firm to grasp on to. Instead, I feel her as an anchoring presence, a woman who did what was right at the time. Was my mother the long pined-for child that brought laughter to Antonella's home? Or was Antonella happily living her life, thank you very much, until her wayward sister-in-law gave her no choice but to play the role of mother?

I go to the bathroom curious to see if I look any different in the mirror. I have more lines on my face, it's true; even a grey hair or two. And the beginnings of those crows' feet I know so well in my mother at the corners of my eyes.

Remembering what Mum told me about her mother makes me angry. The eyes of the woman in the mirror narrow and her lips, open and carefree just months ago, now increasingly pursed, mash together in frustration.

'Why did you do it to her?' I say to my grandmother, my angry words hitting the mirror with such force that the image in front of me splinters and I'm left staring into my own eyes, alone in the bathroom again.

But the truth is I know the answer. She didn't do it to my mother. She did it for herself.

I'll go back to Mum's, look at the photos again. I've built a mental picture of Antonella now: I imagine her the brunette, buttoned-up counterpart to the billowing Marilyn of Nonna Chiara. But only a photograph will tell me if that's true.

First, though, back to Bird. The way all paths lead. The riddle I return to again and again.

Mum is out of hospital. It seems time has not run out for her yet, or at least she's found a way to freeze it through sheer force of will. 'It must be my Sicilian genes,' she says, smiling weakly, as if even her cheek muscles are tired.

I help her home, rolling up the yellow-and-red blanket, stuffing the cooking magazines in a tote bag, the dog-eared copy of *A Room of One's Own*. She walks as if the floor is sticky, as if she can't quite detach her feet from the linoleum. The hospital corridor suddenly seems twice as long, stretching endlessly in a tunnel of strip light after strip light, a dull artificial glow pointing the way to a large window at the end where finally natural light streams through.

In the car, I ask again how she's feeling, though I've already asked multiple times. Suddenly it seems to be the only thing there is to talk about. I don't want to ask her about the past — as much as I want to ask her about my grandmother, I worry she'll sense these are deathbed questions — and yet there is little to say about the future. She won't be getting better — *that* we know.

'Shall I make us some tea when we get back?' I say. The little things in life, I think, that nod to something so much greater. 'I could pick up some cannoli from that bakery you like on the High Road.'

'That would be nice,' she says, and then we're silent once again, row upon row of houses filing by, except of course we're the ones passing the houses, gliding by in Mum's little black Golf.

As I turn the key in the front door, I try to unthink the idea that this is where she will die. Sadness threatens to bubble into hot tears — I help Mum to an armchair and then rush to the kitchen to put the kettle on, afraid that a single word from her will set me weeping, and that's not what she needs now. She needs strength. She needs positivity. She needs smiles. I take deep breaths, counting, thinking of my yoga. As I wait for the kettle to boil, I feel a desperate urge to be back with her, not to waste a single moment of whatever time we have left. I hurry back to the living room and there she is, a shrunken version of herself, already starting to doze. But she must have heard me, because her eyes flutter open and she smiles. 'Isn't that the kettle?' she says, and she's right.

Back to the kitchen again. Separation. Who knows when I'll return to find her gone.

But in the living room, clutching our hot mugs, she seems re-energised. She grins at me conspiratorially, says how lovely it is to be having tea with her daughter.

'I don't know what I'd do without you,' she says.

I want to say the same back, but the words stick in my throat.

I think of Bird, and how Bird needs me. Bird has gone without food for hours. I should be going back to her. Then I hate Bird. I hate Bird for possibly taking me away from Mum. All I want is to be with Mum as long as I can. I wish I could get rid of Bird, though I know I never would. She's too vulnerable. She'd never survive alone. I think of what Doctor Abioye said, about moving in with Mum, being with her more. I'd like to do that. Could I bring Bird with me? I wonder what Mum would say.

Suddenly my whole centre twists tight like rope. I cry out, almost dropping my tea. Mum looks at me, about to ask what's wrong, but the last thing I want to do is worry her. I run out of the room, to the small loo under the stairs, weak at the knees. I clutch the cold lip of the sink, leaning on it as another wave of pain ripples through me. For a moment I wonder if another egg is coming; I sit on the toilet, afraid of what might come out, but also willing my body to evacuate whatever's causing this wrenching pain.

And then it's gone. There's only a dull ache, and the nagging thought that something is wrong.

I return to the living room, conscious I'm still trembling. Mum is asleep, head tipped back, mouth open, her tea cold and half-drunk on the coffee table, her hands clutched oddly on her chest like a Tyrannosaurus.

There's a photo on the coffee table in front of her, A5, with a small yellow Post-it. I pick it up: 'Antonella.' The woman staring back at me is not who I expected at all: she's no less glamorous than Chiara; a brunette, yes, but with bouncy curls, painted lips and a dazzling smile. It's disconcerting – not at all the image of a matronly old maid that society had planted in my mind. In fact, there's something of Meg in her. I consider taking the photograph with me, but then think better of it and put it back, right where Mum had left it. I don't know how many copies she has.

I fish amongst her bags for the yellow-and-red crocheted blanket and drape it around her, tucking in the edges so she'll be nice and warm.

I wonder if anyone will ever do the same for me.

※

As so often happens, seeing Mum sets me thinking about children again. I can't help but think that it would make David happy, despite his protests. He's back in two weeks. I want to do right by him, not string him along.

Safa having Yasmin – and Lisa and that girl Vicky from school and my cousin Ellie and my colleagues and Amanda and Tom and Ravi and Dimitri and Omar – makes me wonder if I should. They all seem so happy, in between complaining about the sleepless nights and the missed social occasions and the fact that holidays are no longer holidays. They show me the pictures: the smiling, the laughing, the cute cheeks that you want to pinch and the funny songs about ladybirds. They hug, they 'whoopee', throwing their children into the air and catching them again. They nuzzle. Truly, they seem content.

But when I try to imagine what it would be like, all I can think about is Bird. Bird, who's sitting here in front of me struggling to eat the seed-and-nut mix I've lovingly prepared. She needs me every morning when I wake up, every time I go out, wherever I am. I can't stop thinking about her, every morning when I wake up, every time I go out, wherever I am.

I wonder more and more when Bird will grow up, make her own way in the world. Because I have the sense that she will. Not like Yasmin, in eighteen years. Soon. The way she looks at me, the way she cocks her head; I can tell she's thinking 'I shouldn't be here. This isn't right. This isn't the place for me.' And one day, I can tell, she's going to leave.

The thought fills me with terror, of course, like the terror at the thought that Mum too will leave me behind, or that David and I might choose different paths and lose each other along the way.

At the emptiness of this house. The days to fill, time flipped from an urgent trickle of sand to an endless desert. And the silence.

But then I remember: I know how to fill the silence. I could travel the world. I could fill it with friends. With songwriting. With joy.

I pick up my phone, and message Meg.

I start to see fertility ads when I look at clocks. The little screen on the microwave warns in bold type that I'm Getting Too Old. The traditional face above the kitchen door tells me that soon my ovaries will dry up. When my radio alarm clock goes off in the morning, the announcer warns that my one-in-a-million chance will be half-in-a-million. David's chance, too.

That the Moment of Truth – the moment to decide – has come.

I start to think that this could all be a farce. My ovaries might have dried up years, decades ago. I might never have been built that way at all.

And then I remember that 'barren' is the lite option. The menthol cigarette. I could be incubating something fatal, running out of time in more ways than one.

I go to my keyboard, open up the publisher's feedback on my phone.

Mortality is motivating.

Mum's recovering well from her stroke. Unusually, the doctors think her symptoms were only temporary. I weep when I get the news, a dam bursting.

She's been given a second chance, and so have I. Now is the time. To decide.

I ask Bird what she thinks. I talk to her at length about the pros and cons. She's still getting stronger, but I can't tell whether she's getting ready to leave, or something else. The way she looks at me, head cocked to one side, reminds me of the time she whistled that eerie tune, and I'm noticing again how pointed her beak is, the sharpness of her talons. I picture her three times her size, ruling the roost, me confined inside for ever, her human slave. I think of lion tamers devoured by the beasts they thought they'd tamed.

But then she closes her eyes and looks harmless. A black bird, nothing more. I feel a kind of sadness, that I'll no longer have a downy head to nuzzle. No longer see something grow and change every day, from chick to almost full-grown bird, species unknown. She doesn't respond to my deliberations, of course, only looks at me – peacefully now – through bird eyes, seeming to say, 'Why worry?'

But I have to worry. As social media tells me, the stakes are too great. The choice between a life that I can't imagine now, but that might offer fulfilment, or a life full of regret, that people tell me will be empty.

I think of Mum, of how painfully I love her, a feeling that my heart could stretch like elastic three times around the globe with its love. I wonder what will happen to that love when she's gone.

Bird looks up at me, expectant.

I should tell David about Bird before he gets back, I really should – say I found Bird in the garden, or the park. But every time I try, the words get stuck somewhere between my brain and my eyes, and never reach my tongue. It's an expensive way to buy time; each time I speak to him feels like a betrayal, the weight of my secret going from violin to cello to bass as the day of his return looms. And yet, as I watch Bird sitting on my old hoodie, shredding the stitches with her beak, I know it's the right decision. This is between me and her – at least while I work out how I feel.

Since I haven't told David about Bird, the first he'll know about her will be when he walks into the living room and sees her in her nest, black feathers contrasting with white linen.

Or maybe he'll sense her presence before that, the way I do every time I come through the front door – not just the rancid smell of her toilet box but a feeling that can't be shaken off, heavy as an ill-fitting winter coat.

I try to imagine what that moment will be like. Will his face light up as he marvels at this miracle of (un)nature? Or will he be horrified, say he wants to leave me, beg me to get rid of her?

I picture him arriving, and I feel calmer, the way I always do when he's around. Suddenly Bird doesn't seem like such a burden. Maybe she can be our little project, the dog we always said we'd get. David will know what to do; straight away he'll be talking about building perches for her in the hallway, finding ways to grow food for her, inventing contraptions for her to ride with us in the car. I see us watching her grow together, measuring her every day (something I've failed to do), and David teaching her tricks. Maybe eventually she'll even say a few words, if she's that kind of bird. 'Music is life,' she caws, making our dinner guests laugh.

But even in this daydream, the novelty starts to wear off. We get grumpy with each other, arguing over who should stay home with Bird instead of attending that wedding in Derbyshire. He says the money for Bird's feed should come from my account, because I'm the one who decided to keep her. Then we agree to share the costs but we argue over whether she really needs that new aviary, and what level of insurance to get. Instead of helping each other willingly, like we always have, life becomes a chit list, of favours owed and outstanding. We stop thanking each other.

'Life is music,' caws Bird, but it no longer makes us smile.

***

It's Jess' wedding day. When my alarm goes off, I immediately flick to the list Jess sent me, pink and flowery on the screen, with all the things I've got to remember to do this morning. I'm not even the maid of honour.

I wouldn't miss her wedding for the world, but I wish it wasn't right now. I still have that email from the publisher burning for a reply. I haven't made enough progress: I've cracked the melody, but the lyrics don't quite fit, stress falling in the wrong places no matter how many times I rewrite.

The first thing is to get dressed and dolled up. I do so with Taylor Swift playing in the background, to get me in the mood. Bird hops around watching me and flexing her wings, unsure of what to make of it. Then she preens herself, copying her mum. I wonder if it's normal that she hasn't flown yet. Maybe I ought to try jumping off the sofa and flapping my arms about to show her how.

I've decided I can leave Bird at home – she's managed when I've been at work, so hopefully she can survive a night alone. It's time to set off, but first I have to crumple up her newspaper like a prank fish-and-chip packet, wrinkling my nose at the smell, stuff it as far down as I can in the bin, replace it with clean newspaper and wash my hands. And then, after

I've left the house, I can't just get the Overground straight to the venue, because I have to go via a florist in Clapham to get Jess' bouquet. God knows why it can't be delivered with the rest of the flowers, or why it has to be in Clapham. Something about the bouquet woman being more expensive.

I get on the train instead and cram in with far more people than I'd expected on a Saturday morning, hoping I don't sweat or crumple my dress.

Several changes later and feeling a little foolish with bouquet in hand, I arrive at the venue, a pub calling itself an Inn in East Dulwich. There are flowers everywhere – so many flowers I almost wonder what the point of the bouquet is. But it's Jess' day and I stop myself from saying anything when I see Cassie, the Maid of Honour, who's been in charge of this feat of logistics.

'Where's Jess?' I ask as she gives me an air kiss on the cheek, wafting perfume my way so that I almost sneeze – though that might have been the flowers.

'In her room, of course. She's expecting you,' says Cassie, and then she dismisses me with a wave of her hand, more interested in where the petunias will go.

I follow a sign past the bar to the rooms and stomp up a carpeted staircase through a warren until I find the 'Blyton Suite'. Someone's stuck up a handwritten card saying 'Jess and Freddie' in loopy writing.

For a split second while I see my hand reaching out, flat-palmed, to push on the door, I get a flash of the time Jess and I were out with Meg, and Jess announced at about nine p.m. that she'd better be getting home, or it wasn't fair on Freddie. It was one of those cocktail bars that's trying too hard, all strip lighting and music no one's heard of.

'Have you not seen him much this week?' I asked.

'Oh, it's not that. I always feel bad when I'm out and he's home alone, you know?'

I didn't know.

'I'm sure he'll be fine. He's probably watching action movies and having a beer,' I said. OK, so it was perpetuating stereotypes, but that's exactly what Freddie is like. 'Stay out a bit longer! It's still early.'

'Go on Jess, just one more…' Meg egged too.

Jess' eyes flicked to the menu and back to her glass. She was clearly tempted.

'It's different for you, Lia. You're used to the whole long-distance thing. You're used to not having David around.'

I bristled at that.

'It's not that different. The real difference is we're still two people. We've not merged into one amoeba like you.'

I regretted saying it. It felt too sharp, the amoeba metaphor too petty. But Jess only blushed contentedly. She'd taken it as a compliment.

So. Into the Blyton Suite. Time to see half the amoeba.

The door swings open and she's all the words brides are supposed to be. Her hair and make-up is nearly done and she's a kind of snow-queen goddess vision standing at the end of a grand four-poster bed. Her movements are still as jerky as ever, her face angular and striking, but today she's a swan, not a heron. And when she lifts her arms in excitement to see me, it's as if she's spreading her wings.

'Here you go, here's the reading,' she says breathlessly, handing me a piece of embossed card. She's already sent it to me, of course, exactly a week ago – enough time to rehearse, but not so much time to forget about it, as she told me, talking me through the plan that day with the binders. I sink on to the silky down bedspread, looking at the words I've agreed to stand up and say later.

It's something about two becoming one. Almost the Spice Girls, but not quite. It's generic and insufficient: I wish I'd written a song after all, though I fear I'd only have fallen short in the attempt.

My nose twitches and I realise the card is scented. I can't wait to read this out in front of a room full of people.

Later, after the vows have been said and the readings read, Jess and I take a break from the crush on the dance floor, in a side room off the main party. A fire burns in the grate, softening the bite of this chill March night, and the contrast from nightclub to country living room has an instant effect on both of us. We sit on the plush chairs, hers velvet, mine leather, letting our shoes drop from our feet and curling our legs underneath us. All we're missing is mugs of hot cocoa; we could be twelve, at a sleepover, ready to gossip about the boys we fancy.

Jess leans towards me, her face aglow with firelight. I think perhaps she's about to wax lyrical about the day, or look ahead to her honeymoon, or thank me again for the reading.

'We're going to start a family,' she says instead, as if continuing a conversation we'd already started.

The usual mix of emotions. First: joy, for her; then a somersault tinged with sadness; then her own face changes to something more faraway and I start inching towards concern, which is more unusual in these situations.

'That's – that's wonderful, Jess,' I say, though if I'm honest I'd thought maybe they would wait a couple of years, settle down as a married couple first – though why would they? They've practically been married since their first date, and besides, we're all running out of time, everyone knows that, and Jess will know it even more than most, probably even has a chart pinned to her bathroom wall, documenting every day that her eggs are degrading.

She's chewing her lip and staring into the fire now. 'What is it?' I ask.

'I just... I know today's not over yet,' she says, glancing back to the lights of the main room as we catch an echo of ABBA. 'But I already know tomorrow I'm going to feel that comedown – that anticlimax. I've been looking forward to this for so long. And after this, what's there to look forward to?' She turns and looks at me with wide, unblinking eyes. 'What's it all for, you know?'

'Is that why you want a baby?' I ask gently, noticing how soft my voice is, wondering if she'll still hear me over three generations singing 'Dancing Queen'.

'I think so,' she says. 'Freddie feels the same. Isn't that why we're all here?'

'There you are!' says a voice from the doorway, and she breaks out in a wide smile, the beautiful bride again, and it's Freddie, caught between the two worlds, half of him dotted with disco lights, the other amber and rosy. 'Aren't you going to dance?'

I can see Meg throwing some shapes behind him. Safa's at home, of course.

'Right with you!' cries Jess, and she's up, giving me a cursory hug and then running on tiptoe, nymphlike, to Freddie at the door, leaving her satin shoes behind.

I stay sitting for a moment, looking into the white-hot heart of the fire. From the dance floor I can hear the strains of something bland and repetitive. I almost decide to go home to Bird. But then I rejoin the dancers, and wonder what I have to look forward to, and why I'm here.

Meg and I get on the Night Tube together. Meg somehow manages not to look any worse for wear, her liquid eyeliner still perfectly framing her glittering eyes, her jet hair still sleek and shiny. I have the strong feeling I've unravelled quite a bit, though my reflection in the carriage window hides all manner of sins.

Somehow, we've ended up talking about babies. I think we started on the wedding, and how lovely it was, then moved on to Jess and Freddie, and when they might have them. I say, 'They'll be popping them out soon, I bet,' and Meg must have detected the ambivalence in my voice because she asks:

'Don't you want them?'

'I don't know. Maybe not. I thought you knew that?'

'I knew you had your doubts. But then you and David – I thought maybe you might have changed your mind. At least you wouldn't be doing it alone.'

'That's true. But still…' I say, looking away down the length of the carriage at the other bedraggled revellers, some more Lia than Meg, and the one or two men dressed implausibly in suits.

'They're not babies for ever, you know,' Meg says. 'They get a bit older and it gets easier. Each year you get a little bit more of your life back.' Neither of us speaks for a moment. I'm unpacking her words. Suddenly:

'You should freeze your eggs,' she says and the train jolts, rocking her back and forth, her emerald eyes wide and staring. 'If you're not sure, you may as well.'

'It's really expensive,' I say, irritable all of a sudden, though I don't know why.

'Not if you donate. I've been looking into it. If you donate they'll freeze half for free. It's quite a good deal,' she says, her words running on in her enthusiasm.

'Are you doing it?' I ask.

'I already have. Look, I might never find someone, but if I do, I don't want it to be too late.'

I'm winded. I marvel that she's never mentioned this before. I marvel that Meg of the 3 a.m. dancing suddenly seems more like Jess, with her spreadsheets and her plans, insuring herself against an undesirable future.

'When does David get back?' she asks. I wonder if she resents me this wasted privilege; remember my friend from HR, so desperate for a child. It's as if I've got the winning ticket and I'm throwing it away. Perhaps she's right, perhaps I shouldn't; perhaps I should take David up on his offer, or at least give my ticket to someone else, donate to atone for my ingratitude.

'This is my stop,' I say.

'Think about it,' she says.

I hug her in an automatic sort of way and jump up, through the sliding doors, and on to the platform. I give her a wave, and her eyes track me as the Tube pulls away.

For some reason I feel guilty. But I feel something else too.

Betrayed.

As I wait for the bus from the station to my flat, Birdward-bound, I try to shake the stickiness of Meg's words. I've never seriously considered egg freezing before. Now that it's been presented as an option I feel as if I should be jumping at the chance. After all, isn't that what I want? More time?

And yet...

Something in me rebels at the idea of keeping my options open. Instead of my eggs I picture myself, frozen in time, limbs frosted stiff with ice, stuck for ever in a tundra-like wasteland of indecision. Perhaps there is something positive in the fact that if you can't decide, time eventually decides for you.

The bus arrives. I take a seat on the bottom deck, behind two girls who are surely too young to have been on a night out, or perhaps it's their first. They're chattering about the boys they danced with, hooting with laughter about the way one of them kissed. Their youth is overflowing.

I imagine what it would feel like if one of them was my daughter. Not a shuddering, slimy chick, nor a snotty-nosed toddler or crying babe in arms. A girl wearing wedges on a night out for the first time, trying desperately to impress her friends. Finding her feet.

As I walk from the bus stop to my house, breath warming in the collar of my coat, I start to imagine my daughter as an adult, in a way that I never have before. She might have my hair, my mother's striking blue eyes.

I don't picture raising her. That part seems too messy, a kind of eighteen-year-or-more chaos I can only dimly countenance.

Instead, I picture her showing up at my door one day, twenty years from now. I'm in my fifties, living my best life and wondering what happened to those eggs I sprinkled away all those years ago.

'Lia? I think I'm your daughter.'

A glimpse at what might have been.

I open the front door. I think that maybe I'll go to the music room, try to improve on a few bars before bed; I can't leave it too long to go back to the publisher. But Bird has found her way on to the upper landing and is peering down at me from between the bannisters, beak poised in smile or frown, I can never tell which.

What is the meaning of meaning? I think as I make my reclining warrior, then flow into downward-facing dog, Bird watching me from her nest. This yoga isn't 'meaning', I know that. It's not something inside of me; I won't find it in my chakra or my chair pose. Meaning is creation. Meaning is contributing; it's donating to good causes and giving your time and making the world a little bit better, or at least not any worse. I think guiltily about Mary next door and when I last did her shopping. I tell myself that as soon as I work out what to do with Bird, or as soon as she's strong enough to go her own way, I'll go back to helping at the youth club.

What is the meaning of meaning?

I think about the word 'wellbeing' while I do my chaturanga. That makes me think of drops of water falling into the stillness below, the way hundreds combine in syncopated harmony, each drop making its singular contribution to the magnificent whole. Of how wells can spring up in the most unexpected places, bringing life in the midst of the desert.

That's meaning.

'Why did you have me?' I ask Mum. We're sitting in her overgrown garden, her face framed by wallflowers, the gentle spring light offering some little warmth to supplement the blankets I've wrapped her in, shoulder to toe. She'd make a beautiful grandmother.

She looks surprised, probably wondering what kind of mood I'm in. She gazes off into the middle distance, maybe wondering if the azaleas need watering. She frowns ever so slightly, though I don't know what about.

Without looking at me, she says, 'I don't think I ever thought about it. Isn't it just what you do?'

'But surely it's the biggest decision anyone will ever make?' I say, feeling as I do so often in these conversations that I'm on some kind of parallel plane, where logic operates differently and everything is back to front.

'Well, if you think of it as a decision, I suppose you're right.'

'Is it only a decision if you don't have them?' I ask.

Suddenly I worry I've hurt her: that I sound ungrateful. 'It's different now. It's harder. I'm sure children must be the same, but society expects more.' She pauses, continues gently. 'Motherhood is a gift. Not everyone can, you know.'

Am I grateful to have been born? I am grateful to be here, in this little garden with its stone walls and its yellow flowers, drinking tea with a mother who is still alive, whose blood flows through my veins.

'I love you,' I say, as if that makes up for it. 'Thank you for everything you've done for me.'

She looks at me a little blankly, as if bemused, as if again wondering what's on my mind. And then she takes my hand in hers. 'I suppose there's something in what they say, too. It's a way to live for ever.' She reaches up and pushes my hair behind my ear, grasps my chin for a few seconds, looking at me with a kind of longing.

Against my will my vision blurs and I feel hot tears on my cheeks.

When I think of Mum leaving me, I can see a hole opening in the ground, so big and wide I might fall into it. Without her I don't know if I'll know who I am or where I'm going. I don't know what I'll do without her love, its constant murmur, its sunset glow.

Maybe that's what I could give a child.

'Now come on, I'm not going anywhere any time soon,' she says, though we both know that depends on your definition of 'soon', and I hurry to cover what I've said, to reassure that's not what I meant, that I was only trying to justify my choices, or at least the choice I'm ever so tentatively thinking of making, though I haven't made my mind up yet, of course I haven't, because I'll probably change my mind, because most women do, because you get to a certain point and wham! your body decides that's what you want, and then before you know it your life has changed for ever.

But sitting in this little overgrown garden with its stone walls and its yellow flowers, the incipient sun warming us ever just a little, I wonder if I want it to.

I meet Meg for brunch at a café on Islington High Road. Shoppers stroll past the window, pondering their spring wardrobes and hunting for treasure. The café is a chain but it tries to sound home-made by calling itself 'Lucy's'. They've got brunch down to a formula: the little flower pot on the table, the unrecognisable muzak in the background, the menu of smashed avocado and milk substitutes. All the waiters wear full-length blue aprons, as if they're about to roll up their sleeves in the kitchen.

We've seen a lot more of each other over the past year, like the first year out of uni when the rest of our circle got these high-pressure jobs and started working long nights and long weekends. Except now it's babies that have them losing sleep.

It's not merely that the rest of our friends have other things to be doing at ten-thirty on a Saturday morning. It's that we're further apart than before, a gap inevitably created as we each take different paths, and in that gap sits all manner of things: the inability to fully comprehend the road the other has chosen; a curiosity that's thirsty; and perhaps the tiniest pinch of superiority, of 'my path is best', that can never fully be erased, at least not from the subtext, no matter how many times we say 'each to their own'.

And here I am with Meg again, ready to dissect her last date like we've always done, except it feels different this time, ever since our conversation on the Tube.

Ironically, we're surrounded by yummy mummies and their babies, presumably at a different stage in the life cycle, or else wealthy enough to live nearby, unhindered by the great migration to the outer boroughs and Home Counties. She navigates past several prams to take her seat, hair black as cast iron hanging in loose ringlets today.

'Most effective form of birth control ever, eh?' she jokes as a nearby baby starts to scream. But I see her emerald eyes linger on them, and remember what she told me on the Tube about finding a partner. I don't know whether to bring it up. It feels inappropriate, somehow. 'How's work going?' I ask. We scan the menu. I flinch at the chicken-wing appetiser, and wonder whether to tell her about Bird. But the moments pass too quickly for me to pick one and settle on it. Once again I wish I had the courage to tell David.

'Have you seen that new show – the one about the dragon breeder?' she asks. I haven't. She tells me about it. Our smoothies arrive. I feel a twinge of pain, but don't mention it. She's relaxed. It would ruin the atmosphere.

'I've had some interest from a music publisher, in one of my songs,' I say, feeling slightly guilty that I'm telling Meg before Safa. 'They're a gateway to the record companies – they pitch your songs for you.'

'Oh Lia, that's *wonderful*!' she says, gesticulating wildly like she's back on the dance floor. 'I can't believe I'm going to have a songwriter friend. Will you bring me as your plus one to the Brits? Pretty please?'

I squirm, change the subject. The trouble with making your hope public is your failure becomes public too.

'How's your mum doing?' she asks. Suddenly I can feel it: pressure mounting, a dam about to burst again.

'Oh, you know…' I drink some more smoothie. I think about how one day soon, Mum's last day will come.

I ask Meg how her last date went. I do really want to know.

'Tragic. Even better birth control,' she says, half-casually, half-bitterly. 'I don't think he understood that if there's only one of you speaking, it's not a conversation: it's a speech.' I laugh in all the right places, but I can't help feeling uneasy. I can see her counting the weeks in her head; the fertility trickling away.

For the first time in a long time, I feel truly lonely.
I start to wonder if Bird is the answer.

⊙

I think about how every egg in your ovaries is a one-in-a-million possibility. How every month, your body gears itself up to host new life. Yes, one of these million could be a person one day, with fingers and toes and thoughts about the meaning of life and capitalism and whether Ant and Dec were ever funny. But an egg alone does not a person make. At school Safa and I thought it was strange. We wondered, if these ova were so special, why people didn't make little gravestones each month, a whole garden of them for a lifetime? We used to call periods being 'in mourning'. We imagined women grieving each month over babies that never were.

But life's not like that. You can't wallow in despair over something that happens twelve times a year. You can't wallow in despair over nothing coming to nothing.

Some might call them unfulfilled promises. Dreams that were never dreamt. Songs that were never sung – no, never written.

Is the world any lesser without them? Or is it only different?

⊙

Bird increasingly seems bored, cawing every time I leave the room and worrying at her towel when I'm there. I've followed advice from the Internet: surrounded her with mirrors and small toys, trinkets from my travels, a Slinky I haven't touched for years, and brightly coloured strings from the craft shop near the station. But it seems she needs me there to move things around for her, so she can scrabble at them with her sharp black beak and ropey red talons, her wings opening wide, filling more and more of the room, lifting her every now and then to hover for a moment above the ground.

Eventually she flexes her wings one more time, folds them around her, tucks her head under one shoulder, and dozes off. I tiptoe upstairs to the music room. A way to live for ever, Mum said. I play my song from start to finish, trying to feel every note as if running my fingers through weaving on a loom. Songwriters don't get the fame, but my keyboard still glitters.

'It's harder than I thought it would be,' Safa writes, in response to my latest 'How are things?'.

I suppose you don't question something you know is going to happen. You don't portion it up into little pieces and then mete them out on the weighing scales, trying to see which side is heavier. You focus on the bigger picture. The smiling photos, the golden retirement. You skirt over all the little details along the way.

I think of Dimitri and how he now responds to my messages – a lot. Mostly to rant, which he says he can't always do to Omar, because 'that'll only drag us both down.' So he sends all his little frustrations to me. 'Maybe it'll help with your decision,' he jokes.

I know Safa doesn't have many friends with babies. She tried to join a local group, but they were full and wouldn't accept anyone else. Her cousins are all in Abu Dhabi and most of our mutual friends have either migrated to suburbia with their barefooted beauties, are still pregnant, or aren't pregnant yet (Jess, and Meg – apparently). Her only yardstick is Instagram, and I worry that could be fatal.

I mention Dimitri to Safa, and Safa to Dimitri. 'Someone to talk to?' I suggest. I arrange lunch at a casual sandwich and salad place I know near Clapham Common. I feed Bird her chia seeds, feeling a little guilty about leaving her alone again, but nonetheless I walk to the café from the station with a spring in my step: two of my best friends, meeting each other for the first time. I worry a little about the dynamic – I hope they'll get along, and it won't feel like I'm having separate conversations with each of them or forcing them to be there ('Look, this is My Friend With a Baby' – as if no one else in the world has one) and then we part ways and they're never in touch again.

I reach the café and spot Safa through the door, past the 'open' sign hanging below my eyeline and the Easter egg stickers dotting the glass. She has Yasmin in the pram next to her. Dimitri is opposite in his black T-shirt and distressed jeans, and they seem to be deep in conversation already. I bound inside, waving and greeting them in a sing-song voice.

'So you found each other!' I exclaim, hugging first Safa and then Dimitri and then leaning down to stroke Yasmin's velvet hair.

'This was such a good idea,' says Safa as I pull out an old wooden school chair. All the tables in this café are those desks we had in primary school, with the inkwells and graffiti carvings still intact. I look down and see that one of the hearts closest to me says 'D+S'. My jollity ebbs away a little.

'We've been comparing notes about colic and—'

'It's crazy really, isn't it, how they just—'

'And you know, if you give them formula before bed it really makes a difference,' says Safa, nodding away earnestly.

'Well... we always give formula!' says Dimitri, and there's an awkward pause before they both burst out laughing.

I try to join in, but I'm beats too late, a different time signature altogether.

'The most important thing is that they're getting fed,' I say, thinking of Bird. They nod and return to comparing notes. I offer to place our orders, leave them to it.

When I get back, Safa trains her hazel eyes on me. 'Lia, I'm so sorry. We've only been talking about babies!'

I smile politely. 'That's OK – that's what we're here for, after all. I'm glad you two are getting along!'

'Tell us about you. What's been going on with Lia?' she says.

'Well...' I look over at Yasmin lying in her cot. I always feel like anything I can think of to talk about is insignificant compared to the act of bringing a creature into being from nothing. Now I've got Bird, of course. But I can't talk about that. 'I've been working on a new song...' Should be working on it right now. Guilt curls around my heart.

'Songs – I meant to ask that, Dimitri,' Safa says, turning to him. 'Do you have any good ones? Because I swear to God, I'm sick of 'Rock-a-Bye!'

'Clean Bandit?' I say, amusing myself with my electropop reference.

Safa looks at me blankly.

'I mean you could sing almost anything to her at that age,' I say. 'Sing whatever takes your fancy!'

'Yes, yes, I could…' she says, murmuring and gazing into her coffee, then continues, almost talking to herself. 'But what I really want to know is what's *best…*'

I start composing a song called 'Mamma Knows Best', then realise with annoyance that Jessie J and Ashton Thomas got there first.

'Relax. Don't put so much pressure on yourself,' I say, trying to seem perky, but Safa keeps looking down at her sandwiches.

'Lia's right. Take it from me, if Mum's happy, Yasmin will be happy,' says Dimitri, leaning forward to take Safa's hand in his.

Safa looks up. This entreaty from another parent has reached deep into her soul. 'Thank you, Dimitri,' she says, looking back at him. 'I really appreciate that.'

I wish I could tell them about Bird.

I keep trying to picture life with David and Bird. For our first anniversary David got me a card with Woody from Toy Story saying, 'You've got a friend in me.' For my second it was 'You and me against the world.' By our fifth, it was a cowboy saying 'Howdy, partner!' I never describe him as my 'other half'; we are both whole. But there are metaphors I like: yin and yang, notes in harmony, cycling tandem.

I try to work out how to tweak these to include Bird. But it all gets thrown off balance.

I'm curled up on the sofa, under a blanket, when I hear the key in the lock. I've been checking my phone every few minutes, looking for updates on David's ETA. I've been picturing his self-conscious smile the moment he walks through the door.

The living room would never make it into a homeware catalogue, but it's my room, and it's just how I like it, within the constraints of practicality, cost and David's tastes, too.

As I wait for David my eyes trace the fragments of the life we've built together. The Whitstable pebble on the coffee table, the dried lilacs on the mantelpiece, from another long walk another time. The bookshelves are mostly about music, with only a few novels but several poetry anthologies. They're good inspiration for lyrics. There's nothing romantic about the sofa, a cream polka-dot nap, but I remember the day we bought it, meandering through IKEA together, playing grown-ups with a kind of glee as if we were in a candy shop rather than the soft-furnishings department.

And then finally the suspended sound of a key in the lock – amazing to think he's been carrying it with him all this time, over all those thousands of miles – and the door opening, feet being wiped on a mat.

I jump up, my blanket falling to the ground, in dramatic folds I imagine but don't look at because I'm already scampering into the hall to where David stands, centre of gravity in the entryway, smiling at me almost sheepishly as if to say, 'I'm sorry it's been so long.'

And then we're kissing, and despite all my talk of being two separate people and going my own way I want our molecules to fuse together, a molten alloy, and we hug and I'm not sure I'll ever let go.

But eventually I do, and he steps back and holds my hands and looks at me, and I too trace his features with my gaze, taking him in in three dimensions after so long seeing him on a screen.

He's different to how I imagined him, and yet the same, tall but light of limb, sure of himself yet lost at the same time.

'Shall we sit down?' he says and smiles at me, and I wonder whether we should be jumping at each other, leaving a trail of clothes through the house like in the movies, but it's OK for that to come later – connection can come first; we need to find each other again.

And so we sit on the sofa, and behind him I can see the space where Bird used to be, and the words are lurking somewhere near my tonsils to tell him, tell him what's happened, but still I know he wouldn't understand, and instead 'I think I don't want children' comes tumbling out like a hasty arpeggio. He raises his eyebrows – this is unexpected – it hasn't even been on his mind.

'Let's talk about it later,' I expect him to say, kick it into the less and less long grass – in fact it's looking so scrubby it can't really hide anything at all – but he doesn't. He holds my gaze, doesn't look away. I feel that somehow, he knows, or guesses – maybe not the feathers, the blood and the gunk, but somehow he can sense what I've been through, and feels my resolve in the way I'm squeezing his hands with mine.

'OK,' he says simply, as if it were a coda, as if it's the end of a sonata we've been writing for some time.

'What if you change your mind?' I say.

And then I wake up in the cold morning light of my bedroom and hear Bird cawing for me downstairs.

I press my face into the pillow, clench my eyes until I see stars.

I've finally got a song I'm happy with. I only hope the publisher likes it, and then the label. I listen to it one last time, then share the file, throwing a stone to skip or sink. No disc to send, no postman to blame for any delay hearing back. He's got it, seconds after I've sent it, and a piece of my soul along with it, zipped into 3.5 MB. Now all I can do is hope.

Mum rings me. She says she wants to go for a walk; it's rare she wants to leave the house, so I can't say no. I leave my scribbled sheet music, leave Bird playing with her bouncy ball, leave my laundry half-hung and head straight over to hers.

As I find her jacket and help her put on her hat, she watches me, as if tracing every line of my face. I feel a twinge, but think I manage not to wince.

'Is something wrong, Lia?' she asks. I have to blink and turn away so that she can't see my eyes watering. I should have known I'd never be able to hide this from her for long. The hospital has asked me to go in tomorrow. Not for her. For me.

'I wish you'd tell me, *cara*,' she says.

But I'm the one who has to worry about her now, and I won't have it the other way around.

Cancer, cysts, endometriosis, it's-all-in-my-head. Daughters shouldn't go before their mothers. It's against the natural order of things.

Too much of what I could tell her is against the natural order of things.

'Thank you for helping me,' she says, and there's the weight of years in her words. 'You're all I ever needed, Lia.' I can tell that she means it.

'Come on, the sun's coming out,' I say, and though I give her her cane, she leans into me, and then we step, arms linked like schoolgirls, out into the white.

FLEDGING

The gynaecology clinic is cold. The room looks like every other doctor's office I've ever been in: the floor a kind of hard resin, mysteriously with small flecks in it that catch the light as if someone wanted to jazz the place up; posters reminding us not to drink or smoke or eat too much red meat; a desk scattered with Post-its; a bed with its fresh tissue-paper sheet; a chair that reminds me of school. More distinctively, there is a plastic model on a corner table: a disembodied, bisected womb, like a kidney bean in shape and colour, with an upside-down foetus nestling inside.

'Take a seat,' my latest doctor says. She's neither male nor pale nor particularly curvy. She's a slim woman of South-East Asian heritage with a leopard-print headscarf. She's a little bit more abrupt than I'd like, but she holds my gaze without looking away and she seems to know what she's doing.

I'm so tired my eyes are heavy in their sockets. I've been up all night, mind going round the circle of life.

I rest the wicker basket on the floor next to me, but don't stop gripping the handle, knuckles white. I try not to look at the womb.

The doctor looks at me and at the basket, and I think I see her narrow her eyes, just for a second, so slightly I can't be sure she did. Does this mean it's bad news? Or is she merely wondering what I've brought?

Her eyes are wide and kohl-rimmed, and her lips smile nervously with bright-pink lipstick as she adjusts her headscarf and readies her notes. She seems businesslike but approachable, and I imagine her going home to a little son and daughter, telling them to do their homework, then playing with them all evening. She's about my age.

'So,' she says.

'So,' I repeat, hand still on the basket.

At this point, I'm sick of the carousel. I know what she's going to say: I need more tests. I can feel it in the room, the way its edges vacillate. A room with answers would be solid. A room with answers would be square and straight.

But I won't take questions for my answer. I've waited long enough, and now I need to know.

I've brought Bird, wrapped in her old white towel, hidden inside this picnic hamper.

The doctor will be horrified. God knows what she'll think I've been up to. But I feel like showing her is the only way to get to the truth. Somehow, I feel that if she sees Bird, she'll be able to tell me what to do. Somewhere on her shelf, in one of those big heavy books, there'll be a protocol to follow. I can't be the only one.

But I don't get a chance to open the wicker lid.

'We've got the results of your tests,' she says. Even as I recoil from the way the room thrums with questions, she seems to want to wade into them, stumbling through the bog. 'We've identified the problem.' This is new. This is unexpected. The room still quivers, and I don't know what to make of it. For a moment I allow myself to hope. I sense

Bird hoping with me, still in her basket. Perhaps clarity will come, after all.

I brace myself, ready to hear the onslaught, the intricate details, the impenetrable medical jargon. My hand breaks contact with the basket, hovering in empty air.

'You have a rare condition.'

I want to laugh. I picture Bird and myself at home, laughing and laughing for hours until we cry.

'It's good news,' she says. 'It's curable. You're going to be fine.' She breaks into a broad smile. I wonder if she means she can make Bird disappear.

Still, one of the knots in my brain comes undone. I feel lighter, more able to think about the future without wondering if I'll be here to see it.

'I'm afraid you'll have to undergo a slightly complicated procedure. Nothing too invasive, but the recovery time will require a two- to three-week stay in hospital.'

Two to three weeks? I'm surprised she's so matter of fact. I start to worry what I'll do with Bird.

'What will they do?'

'It's a little uncomfortable, that's all. Well, forty-seven per cent of patients describe the operation as painful, but it's really very low-level pain, and that will only last a few weeks too. Some patients have noted the pain persisting for longer, but this is rare.'

Before I know it, she's reeling off the side effects. Most sound like the usual you could read on the label of any over-the-counter pill packet – headaches, migraine, vomiting and diarrhoea. Then, amongst the list of side effects, I hear the word 'prolapse'.

'Pro- *what*?'

'It's a risk, but it's a very manageable condition. You may be aware that a significant number of women develop it as a complication of childbirth anyway, particularly in later years,' she says with a small wave of her hand before turning to her screen. 'We can book you in for… September?'

'That's six months from now.' I feel salt pricking my eyes. When she said it was curable I thought I'd be saying goodbye to this pain. Still the side effects cycle in my head, a riff that won't go away.

'I'm afraid we have a long waiting list,' she says. Then for the first time she really looks at me, and I think I see some spark of sympathy. 'Look, here's all the information,' she says, passing me a leaflet so carefully it might have been an ancient papyrus. 'We can prescribe you some stronger pain relief in the mean time.'

I look down at the folded piece of paper, unsure if I really want to read about vaginal prolapse when it feels as if I don't have a choice either way. But I'm confused by what I see.

'It says here there are two options. Why can't I do the one which only takes a day and doesn't list all those side effects? No pain. No waiting list. No recovery time.'

'Oh, I wouldn't advise that,' she says hastily. 'We usually only suggest it for older patients. Women in their fifties.' She twitches as if she wants to snatch the paper back but is prevented by professional propriety.

'It doesn't say that on the sheet,' I press. 'How quickly could I get *that* one?'

'Lia,' she says, pressing her lips together, as if by doing so she can squash her words and therefore soften the blow. And then very quietly, as if telling me someone has died, she says, 'That option causes sterility.'

The funny thing is, now she's said it I can see it there in bold type – the first side effect. In fact, they've devoted two whole lines to it, far more than to anything else, and have even taken the trouble to specify in underlined lettering that this will be I-R-R-E-V-E-R-S-I-B-L-E. And yet my eyes skipped over it. I read it, noted it and moved on. I barely paused.

I feel like I've dived from the concrete edge and opened my eyes underwater to see the world in sparkling crystal. The thrumming stops. With this simple piece of paper, she's made herself the oracle I was seeking, but what she's revealed isn't some external truth. It was inside me all along, eternal as Eve.

'I'll take it. That one, please,' I stammer, the words stumbling in their hurry to escape.

Her eyes pop and her eyebrows dart up as if they've touched a hot stove. I wonder how many times she's had to tell women they can't conceive. I wonder how many women have sat here in this chair, the anguish they must have felt. I think of Meg, lacking her means to an end, yearning for a guarantee. I ought to be in despair.

'Are you OK?' she says tentatively. I rearrange my face a little, try not to smile. A smile is the last thing she expected. Perhaps she thinks I've gone manic. 'This would be irreversible,' she says, drumrolling the word around her mouth, enunciating as clearly as she can, as if she thinks I'm stupid. 'It would be quite unorthodox to carry that out on someone of your age.'

'Isn't it up to me?' Suddenly I feel like she's my mum, telling me I don't have permission to go on the school trip.

'We have a duty of care. We have to make sure you're making an informed decision, that you're not too young to take this permanent step.'

Now my own eyes strain against their sockets.

'A month ago they said I was geriatric.'

'It's a huge decision,' she says, more gently now. 'At least think about it. Think what you'd be throwing away.'

I gaze past her, out of the window where the clouds are thinning and the light has turned from grey to white.

I think of what Mum said. *A way to live for ever.* I think of Bird when she was a shuddering chick, reaching for the light.

The thrumming picks up again, softly at first, then as strong as before. I have the peculiar sensation of being more conscious of having a womb than I've ever been in my life. But it's nothing like the plastic mock-up in the corner. Instead I feel as if there's a cavern opening inside me, picture myself like one of those Greek amphora, an empty vessel echoing and cobwebbed. I see myself as an old woman, crying out in the night to no one. I see my friends with their families at Christmas, David and I splitting up, turkey sandwiches sticking to the roof of my mouth.

I hear Bird shifting in her basket and the doctor glances towards it, eyes widening again. The thrumming is getting louder and louder.

'Do you have any questions?' the doctor asks, seemingly about to ask me what I've brought. But the only questions I have are for myself.

I hear a small squawk, try to mask it with a cough, my breath quickening, heart hammering.

'Ultimately, it's your choice,' she says.

The word 'choice' thunders in my skull. Choices are gifts, I know that; a luxury few can afford. But hidden beneath their shiny wrapping lie responsibility and regret. I think about the regrets I'm being offered today.

I gather my things: raincoat, umbrella, picnic hamper containing impossible bird, and rush out of the room, leaving the kidney bean and the doctor behind; clattering down the hallway and then down the stairs, I make my way out of the warren of the hospital, down abandoned side stairways that no one uses, through corridors with gurneys and past nurses with clipboards, until I emerge from the shadows into the light.

It's overcast but dry. I pant as I walk, feet slapping the pavement, trying to get as far from the hospital as I can, but encumbered by the basket, which prevents me weaving in and out of the crowds. After a few streets I feel a buzz in my pocket. I pause, put down the basket, wondering if it's David. Or Mum. It's an email, and the subject line sets my hand shaking. It's a response to my last message to the music publisher.

It'll only be another question, I tell myself. *He won't have found a label yet.* For a minute I stare at the little notification window, unwilling to open it. Until I open it, I can believe it's good news. Until I open it, I can hear the stadium roar, see the song soaring in the charts, picture the platinum record on my wall.

I know there'll be other chances after this. It's not now or never.

But I so want it to be now, with a primal aching.

I tap the email.

The preamble sentences don't reassure me. When it's good news, there's no preamble. And yet…

I read on, aware of nothing but these black typed letters.

I'm sorry that this news will come as a disappointment. Have you considered a publishing library? The tune might make a good jingle.

Well, that's that then.

He makes it sound like I've done this hundreds of times before.

Like this was one song amongst many, part of my dazzling repertoire.

Like it'll be easy to just pick another song and run with it.

I do have other songs. Of course I do. And there are other publishers.

But I was sure this song was special. I even had some perfect artists in mind. I'd allowed myself to think that this might actually be my break.

Never allow yourself to picture it. It's so much harder when it's taken away.

There's a squawk. I look up, towards the rooftops, then I remember Bird is here at my feet. Stuck in her wicker basket. I bend over, my shoulders hunching. Close my fingers around the wicker handle, brittle and crunchy. Whisper to Bird under my breath. I'd sing my song to her, but it's too painful. And though a part of me is glad she's here, I know she can't make me feel better.

I pick up the basket and start to walk again.

The choice the doctor has presented me with still careers around, tipping from one side to another and back again like the screeching of a possessed see-saw in a haunted playground.

Without conscious thought, I find myself heading towards the park. Funny how the feet know where to go without direction from the head. I need an open sky, air that's green, and enough quiet to hear my own thoughts.

When I get there, the cacophony in my brain calms a little. Sycamores stretch to the heavens and lush grass blankets the ground.

Bird is still in her basket, and she's squawking more loudly with each step I take. I stop, kneel beside the path in the riotous lawn and start to undo the fastenings on the wicker. Finally, the lid swings open, Bird's eyes meet my own, and she's silent.

She looks less dishevelled than before. Two months after hatching, her feathers no longer stick up at odd angles, and she no longer looks fresh-from-the-egg slick, but instead shiny and lush. For the first time she looks like a bird, not a chick.

She caws at me from the basket, gently this time, and I remember she's never truly tasted fresh air, never seen how high the sky reaches.

From my kneeling position I whistle at her, a single note. She starts to whistle back, and this time I recognise the tune. I can't help smiling – it's 'Goodbye Yellow Brick Road', shrill but clear.

Perhaps there's something of me in her after all.

Without thinking I extend my hands into the basket, and she steps on to them, one spiny foot after another, perches, comfortable and ready to be carried. She's lighter than I remember.

And then I sing with her. Like Snow fucking White.

She whistles back to me, then looks up at me with amber eyes, cocking her head. It's crazy, but I feel like she's trying to tell me something.

At once I know what to do.

The clouds move and broad sunlight streams down, illuminating the purple tips of her wings. By the swings children are playing, their shouts boisterous and gleeful. *Vinni la primavera*; spring has come. I can feel its call. So can she, it seems. She turns her head to the sky, where a lone bird – I don't know what kind – crosses our vision. And then she's flapping her wings and somehow, even though I never showed her how, she's away.

I feel a great tug as my heart sinews stretch like elastic and then snap. I cry out; it feels as if Bird is taking a part of me with her. But then I take a deep breath, clutching at my chest, and I'm still here, all of me, from the squishy soft flesh of my palms to the pressure in the balls of my feet.

Near the trees at the edge of the park Bird falters, and I wish I could go to her, hold her tight, feel her warmth against my face again. But then her instincts kick back in. Her newly strong wings flap as if they've always done this, and before I know it she's flying away past the chimney tops, getting smaller and smaller, heading straight up into the open sky, eager to explore the world. The clouds far behind her. A black speck against the blue.

Free.

It's time to go. I have songs to write, places to be. Doctors to call.

I pick up the empty basket and turn my steps towards home, with its music room and goldfinches in the garden. My empty nest.

Every baby born is a miracle. Every baby born is a gift. That's what they tell me, and I know that for them it's true.

I can see it now: the hospital room flooded with sunlight, doctors crowded around, a small breakable thing held high as if from Pride Rock, tears in everyone's eyes.

But I also know there are other miracles. Trees silhouetted against the sun on a March morning. Cocooning yourself in duvets when you know you have nowhere to be. Dancing until your feet hurt and the lights come on, the ecstasy of letting go. Following where the wind takes you. Dreaming without limit.

I see a long path stretching behind and ahead of me. At every fork I've known, deep down, which one to take, but all along the way there've been people calling my name, offering me immortality, wisdom, love that knows no equal. Now the path is straight, and quiet, and I feel sure something important lies at its end.

It's as if someone has snatched a book from my hands, a book that I've been reading for a very long time, and skipped forward to the ending and read it aloud.

A part of me feels sadness for the pages I didn't get to read. For the alternative endings I could have had.

But as if a switch has flipped, I feel a smile break out on my face and – I barely dare admit it – relief rushes through me. It's totally unexpected, as if I've been walking a tightrope this whole time, holding my breath, and only now can it escape and be free, into the fresh air, past the trees. My questions follow after this great exhalation, dispersing like dandelion seeds on the breeze. Everything in the park seems brighter, the edges sharper, as if someone, somewhere has turned up the contrast.

I message David: *Can't wait to see you. Good news at the doc.* He sends me a picture of him grinning on top of a skyscraper. *That's the best thing I've heard in months.* I feel a twinge of guilt: I know there's more to say, things that I'll have to explain. But I'd rather gauge his reaction in three dimensions.

The publisher said no, I write. *But I won't stop believing.*

Maybe later I'll go for a run, then pop next door to Mary, bring her some cupcakes. I'll visit Mum and ask her about Antonella, and tell her how David's last concert went. Maybe I'll save a few cupcakes for Safa, stop by to see her and Yasmin this evening – Yasmin with her little grin, eyes wide as the universe, fingernails like fragments of eggshell, and fingertips that curl around mine.

I wend my way through narrow streets of cobblestone, following my feet down detours I've never seen. I don't know what time it is, but it doesn't matter. I have all the time in the world.

I message Jess, Safa and Meg. *Dinner on Saturday?*

The replies follow fast from the blue ticks. *I'm there – Sure – Awesome.* xxx. A chorus of heart emojis. *Love you guys.*

I start to hum – a new tune that needs only words.

ACKNOWLEDGEMENTS

At my first major author panel, we were asked whether we agreed with the phrase 'to birth a book'. I explained that I felt conflicted. I've used it tongue-in-cheek for this book on numerous occasions, but that's just because I'm a fan of eggcellent puns. And I do like the idea it conveys: this is something important to me. This took time, thought and love. *This* is my legacy. On the other hand, I answered that I worry the phrase itself reinforces the idea that women must, one way or another, birth SOMETHING – be it baby, egg or book! – which is, of course, very much an idea that *Fledging* seeks to deconstruct.

I wanted to open my acknowledgements with 'they say it takes a village'. Then Google told me that tons of people have already used that phrase, in acknowledgments for books, PhD theses… etc. But those projects were not necessarily as intimately linked with the theme of raising a child as my book, so I've decided it is the right phrase, and I'm going to use it anyway.

They say it takes a village to raise a child – well, books take a village as well…

THANK YOU

First to my family. I don't remember what first made me want to be an author, because I have wanted to be one since I can remember, but I have the sneaking suspicion my Aunt Ingrid had something to do with it. Thank you for your undying encouragement – and for still bringing up that short story about the telephone, twenty-five years later. To my mum, my most avid reader, for making it through more drafts of my novels than anyone else, and being one of the best editors I could have asked for. For tweedle dee and tweedle dum. To my dad, for my terrible sense of humour, for turning everything into a song, and for teaching me to go after my dreams. For your (very original) adventures of Jonathan Livingstone Seagull. To both of you, for teaching me to think for myself, and for being so respectful of our choices – for this, also to Martine and Stephen. To my brother, for storytelling games by the fireside that went onandonandon, for the games and the silliness. To Aslak for being one of my first readers, and to Cecilie for the publishing advice. To Tina, Grete and the Gjendals for showing me it's not only DNA that counts. And of course, to Giles, for far too many things to list here, but above all for being a true partner in all things, for taking my writing seriously, and for helping me to take it seriously too.

Second must come the Southbank Scribblers: Matt and Pippa. This book truly would not exist without you. Thank you for making me a better writer, for sharing the ups and downs, for the friendship, the DIY writing retreats, the sudden last-minute consultations, and, most of all, for reading the opening chapter and telling me to keep going.

Third, to the midwives of the publishing world (in chronological order): to Natasha Bell for her excellent teaching at City Lit; Reflex Press for giving me something better to say in my query letter; Aina, for your feedback; to Damien for being the best champion anyone could ever have, and Jess and the whole Indie Novella team for your editorial support. Thank you especially to Laetitia for taking the plunge, for helping me find Chiara and Antonella, and for pushing me to do the best I possibly could on every word. To Ciara for answering all my little questions. And finally to Will, for your enthusiasm, vision, the stunning cover (in just the right shade), for the many emails and DMs, the cracking puns, and for being the one to make this book a real, physical, ink-and-paper reality.

To everyone else who took the time to read my drafts and made *Fledging* what it is today: Cecilia, Kate, Khema, Charlotte, Lily, Fran, and childfree cheerleaders Nicole Louie, Kristen Tsetsi and Ali Hall. (Plus Emma Duval and Merle Bombardieri for the encouragement – and Jennifer Flint and Bobby Palmer for the eggstra special solidarity!)

To others who inspired and continue to inspire me, including Sheila Heti (*Motherhood*), Ann Patchett ('everything was designed for this one thing: I wanted to write'), Rebecca Solnit ('But there are so many things to love besides one's own offspring, so many things that need love, so much other work love has to do in the world'), Amy Tan ('what's in me that I'd have wanted to pass on is already in the books'), Megan Daum (*Selfish, Shallow and Self Absorbed*), Therese Shechter (*My So-called Selfish Life*), Ruby Warrington (*Women Without Kids*), Farrah Storr ('I often tell people that I don't have a child shaped hole in my life; I had, for a short time, a purpose shaped hole in my life') and Christine Erickson (New Legacy Institute).

To the friends who helped inform Lia's journey, whose words helped germinate this story. To the wonderful friends and family who have supported my writing journey, not just *Fledging* but the manuscripts that came before it. To the dear friends who are mothers themselves, for understanding, and for bringing my Yasmins into this world. You all know who you are.

Fledging is dedicated to…
All those who want children, but can't have them
Who don't want them, but don't have the privilege of choice
But most of all to those who needed to see themselves in these pages.
I hope you did.